WENDIGO NIGHTS

WENDIGO NIGHTS

Benjamin Coward

Benjamin Coward
Gainesville, Florida
USA

Benjamin Coward
Gainesville, Florida
USA

This book is for all the outsiders.
Please remember your life has worth.

CHAPTER I

Amanda was running for her life. She had never been so scared before. Her heart hammered like staccato drumbeats. The stitch in her side made her take ragged breaths.

How could she keep going? There was no way. This was a nightmare. The woods around her were black as night could be. She ran into a spider web all of a sudden and clawed frantically at her face. Then she tripped over a root and fell hard on her side.

Looking around wildly, she tried to remember which way she was headed. Had she spun around when she grappled with the spider web? Why had she ever chosen to come out to the middle of nowhere with Chris?

It had been exciting sneaking out to be with a hot guy like Chris. He had said in a confident voice, "I know the perfect spot. No one will disturb us. Plus, who the hell cares if two teens drive to a nearby wood for some action?"

That's how he had said it, "action," like their clandestine, fun times were just a game. Though, at the time, she hadn't complained. It felt good to kiss him, his tongue against hers and his hand finding all the sensitive spots. They had been so close to actually doing the deed.

Then suddenly, the old Saturn's front door had crashed open. Chris was ripped from her arms and disappeared screaming into the night. Blood had sprayed her face, making her close her eyes as she tried to find the door handle. Amanda had heard bones breaking and flesh tearing along with Chris's frantic pleas for help.

Amanda didn't wait to see what was happening. She threw open her own door and ran for the woods, hoping to find somewhere to hide. Behind her, she heard an unearthly roar and scratching of claws on metal as whatever it was that was attacking tore its way over the car to get to her.

Now here she was in the middle of the woods, covered in blood. She hurt all over from the scratches she had gotten running blindly through the trees and underbrush. Out of breath and terrified, she inhaled deeply and cried out, "Please, someone help me!" She made to run on but was not able to see and tripped again.

Amanda spun as she fell, landing hard on her back and striking her head on a rock protruding from the ground. She tried to pull herself to her feet, but she was too dizzy to stand. Her head pounded, and tears streamed down her face along with blood from her cracked skull. She began to crawl.

"Please, God! Someone help me!" she screamed again, so loud she heard her voice break. Then she stopped. Something had changed. Amanda took a breath, trying to calm herself and decide what had gotten her attention. She realized the woods around her were silent, and it was instantly freezing cold. It was as though she had lost all hearing in the middle of winter. For a moment, she wondered if the silence meant someone had heard her.

That has to be it. Someone heard me and scared the monster off. And now that person is looking for me to help me. I've got to let them know where I am, she thought. Grabbing a low tree branch and pulling herself up, she breathed deeply again before calling out, her voice shaking from adrenaline, "I'm here. I can't see, and I hit my head."

With a rush, something hit her hard from behind. Amanda felt herself flying forward. Then everything went black.

CHAPTER 2

Jonathan Campbell walked into school and looked about curiously. Everyone was talking more animatedly than usual, which was saying something for kids in high school. But with the news this morning, which his parents had watched raptly, who could be surprised? Two students in senior year had been found dead at Sodalis Nature Preserve.

His parents' worried faces had made Jonathan a little nervous. He hadn't been friends with either Chris or Amanda. Chris had been an arrogant jock and a jerk, while Amanda was a cheerleader. *And everyone knows what those people are like,* Jonathan thought to himself.

Suffice it to say that seniors like the jock and cheerleader didn't run with junior-class nerds like Jonathan and his band of friends. Jonathan was actually quite fond of being thought of as a nerd. In fact, hadn't someone smart once said, "The nerds will run the world," or something like that?

Jonathan saw his two friends sitting next to his locker, waiting for him. Jonathan was the tallest of the group by far, with long legs and arms, brown hair, and dark-brown eyes. Cory waved to him, grinning happily, his braces catching the light. Cory was short, very short, with dark hair and hazel eyes. He was always correcting everyone with what he thought of as the facts. "How can I allow ignorance to go on so blatantly in the world without trying to correct people's misguided and undereducated views?" he had said to Jonathan one day after correcting a football player five times in earth science.

As Jonathan reached his friends, Trevor jumped to his feet and slapped five with him in greeting. Trevor was, well, average—not too tall or short—with brown hair and deep-blue eyes. He was shy and didn't talk much; however, he had always stood as a buffer in the friend group, hearing both sides of an argument and bringing everyone together in the end.

"Hey, man, I guess you heard the news," asked Trevor.

"It's hard not to," answered Jonathan, sitting down and giving Cory a fist bump.

"My mom was going crazy. It was like she thought I would go missing or something too. However, as far as I am concerned, I don't fit the statistics for runaway kids," said Cory, laughing.

"Everyone is so bummed out. I mean, those two died doing something stupid. It's like it's a huge surprise that bad things can happen to people," said Jonathan quietly. In his opinion, he had no remorse for two delinquents who chose to break rules and paid the price.

"Guys, come on," said Trevor in a forceful tone, which was rare for him. Jonathan and Cory both raised their eyebrows at him. Trevor continued, exasperated, "What if it had been one of us that had died, or someone in our families? Have some common decency and respect!"

Jonathan looked down, abashed. Then he had an idea. "But it wasn't us. And you know what I think?"

"What?" both Cory and Trevor asked, Trevor with a bit of trepidation.

Jonathan lowered his voice more, and the three leaned together. "I think this is worth investigating."

Both boys gave Jonathan quizzical looks, and Trevor said, "That sounds dangerous and illegal."

"He's right. It could be seen as tampering with a crime scene," said Cory automatically.

"Listen, haven't you guys heard all the rumors that are already sprouting?" asked Jonathan.

All three boys grew silent and looked around them. People all over were talking about it. They could hear one group of girls sobbing, "It's not fair! It isn't right! Amanda was so nice." And one guy in a group of jocks nearby said, "I don't know what we're going to do without Chris; he's been our ace receiver. The guy could catch anything and run like hell, man."

In a larger group of boys, someone said loudly, "It tore them both up!" Another boy piped up, "My dad said it must have been some type of animal." Finally, one girl huddled in a group of freshmen said nervously, "My parents don't want me to walk home alone. They think it's probably some freak living out in the woods."

The three friends looked back at each other. "Well, what do ya think?" asked Jonathan.

"As far as a freak in the woods, I would disagree. We would have heard something definitive from the police warning people of an escaped inmate," said Trevor.

"And there have been no major predators endemic to Missouri since the last mountain lion was killed in 1927," supplied Cory.

"Exactly," said Jonathan before continuing excitedly, "so, what if it's a cryptid?"

Both boys gave Jonathan skeptical looks.

"I don't know of any cryptids in Missouri—ghost stories for sure, especially around the St. Louis area, but not one of our cryptids," said Trevor.

The three boys loved cryptids and anything supernatural. The idea of finding a new species or unexplainable event was exciting.

"But, what if it is one? This could be our chance," Jonathan half begged.

Cory and Trevor smiled nervously. Jonathan knew they couldn't pass up an opportunity like this right in their back yard, so to speak.

"All right, but we have to come up with a good plan to investigate," said Cory.

Trevor nodded, adding, "Yeah, one where we don't get caught and arrested."

CHAPTER 3

By lunchtime, Jonathan had come up with a plan. The three boys grabbed their trays, and as always, Jonathan grabbed a piece of greasy pizza from the tired-looking lunch lady. Then he headed to a table at the back of the crowded lunchroom, every now and then stepping over people's legs that would just happen to stick out into his path.

While he waited for his friends, he pulled up maps on his phone of both the city of Hannibal and Sodalis Nature Preserve. The preserve was large; it was, in fact, Hannibal's second largest park with over two hundred acres. Situated on the south side of the city, just to the west of Lover's Leap and the Mississippi River, the preserve could be accessed from Ely Road. However, Bear Creek also ran through the park.

Trevor sat down with his lunch of a grilled cheese sandwich. Soon after, Cory sat down with his own piece of pizza and began trying to blot up the overwhelming amount of grease from it.

"So, what did you find out?" asked Cory without pretext.

"Here, take a look," answered Jonathan, enlarging the map of Hannibal.

The boys leaned forward and gave Jonathan doubtful looks.

"Look at it," said Jonathan wearily. Then he explained, "If we go down Main Street, we can follow Bear Creek right into the preserve without having to use Ely Road."

"That makes sense," said Cory, taking small bites of his pizza.

"As long as you both are sure," added Trevor nervously.

"Of course it will be all right," answered Jonathan.

"Yeah, if we follow the creek and never see anybody blocking the main entrance, we could claim ignorance and that we're just walking down the creek. People do it all the time. That path along the creek is a very popular walking path," said Cory.

Trevor bobbed his head once, giving his friends a weak nod of affirmation.

Then a sing-song voice broke up their plans: "Look, guys, the wittle gay nerds are planning a slumber party." With that, a big, meaty hand grabbed Jonathan's phone.

"Hey, give that back," demanded Jonathan, launching himself to his feet. His abuser, a jock named Jack, ignored him, looking at the phone screen with an amused grin.

"He said, 'Give it back,'" roared Trevor, making a lunge for Jonathan's phone. However, another bully, Chad, pushed Trevor from behind, sending him down hard.

"I'll call the teachers," whined Cory.

The bullies laughed, and Jack tossed the phone onto the table, where it landed in Jonathan's half-eaten pizza. People around the lunch-room were starting to take notice, many of them breaking into laughter.

"Be seeing you," winked Jack. With that, the jocks began to walk off, and Jonathan watched them go. As always, he hadn't been able to do a thing; he had frozen up, too much of a coward to stand up to the bruisers. His frustration was near boiling.

Jonathan tried to ignore the laughter around him and the burning in his eyes as he helped Trevor to his feet. "Thanks for trying to help," whispered Jonathan to his friends.

"It's what we're here for," winced Trevor.

"Yeah, he's right," said Cory, handing Jonathan back his phone, which Cory had taken the time to clean off.

"Let's get out of here," said Jonathan, his head down as he led his friends out of the lunchroom.

CHAPTER 4

The rest of the day seemed to drag on and on. Jonathan was a model student and normally loved his classes. However, even history and earth science seemed boring today. He wanted to be anywhere else and couldn't stop thinking of all the possible cryptids he knew of and the ramifications of finding a cryptid and proving it was real. Such things were not unheard of.

There were so many cases; he found himself running through the list. There was the black-footed ferret that was thought to be extinct until a farmer's dog killed one. The same was true of the bush dog, which was the last of its family tree and was rediscovered deep in the South American rainforests. To go bigger, it wasn't until recently that the colossal squid was proven to be real. Sometimes assumed to be the kraken of mythology, it had previously been thought to be only a legend, a story that drunk sailors told in taverns after difficult times at sea.

How could science be so blind to possibilities? *Closing your eyes to a theory without researching it yourself is just lazy,* thought Jonathan. Then he blinked; he had nearly nodded off—unheard of for him. Blushing, Jonathan realized Mrs. Miller was discussing the Declaration of Independence. "We hold these truths to be self-evident, that all men are created equal," she quoted, her beautiful blonde, curly hair bouncing playfully.

Jonathan frowned. It was a well-known quote. However, the words had only been meant for white men, and only the men. He liked Mrs. Miller. Most of the guys, including himself, had a crush on the petite, vivacious woman. Nevertheless, the hypocrisy of the statement always got to him, and he blurted, "Except that the Declaration goes on to point out that the Native Americans were savages and therefore not equal to white men."

His friends groaned. They knew how Jonathan felt, but Jonathan usually knew better than to interrupt.

Mrs. Miller frowned, saying with heavy disappointment in her voice, "Mr. Campbell, please go out in the hallway. You are being disrespectful and are disrupting this class."

Jonathan got to his feet and headed out of the room, his face red. He sat down in the hallway behind a desk that stayed there for the purpose of separating those who were being disruptive. Also, it was there for people like Jonathan with ADHD who needed a quiet place to take tests. His attention was easily swayed by outside stimuli, making it hard to concentrate. Whenever a student would get up to turn in their test or even fidget, he would feel the pressure to finish quickly. So it made it harder and harder. He would find himself taking glances at the clock and its quick regression of remaining time.

At the squeak of the classroom door opening, Jonathan looked around to see a concerned Mrs. Miller. Jonathan cast his eyes down, slightly embarrassed of his outburst. A twinge of anger still existed, though. How could she teach something that was so inherently misguided? Sure, later on Dr. Martin Luther King, Jr., would use it in his speeches. However, due to the interpretation that Native Americans were savages, it still made people like Jonathan, with Native American blood, like second-class citizens. *Why does the school system only tell part of the truth and ignore others willingly? And why do I get punished for speaking out?*

Jonathan felt his eyes go moist and blinked to get rid of his tears.

He examined his shoes, doing his best to bring them back into focus and not to completely break down. Then he felt Mrs. Miller's nails on his back, scratching gently in circles. It was a secret Jonathan's mother had told to the teacher. "If you ever want him to calm down, do this," he had heard his mother say, time and again. Jonathan felt himself positively melt.

Then, Mrs. Miller was speaking earnestly next to him. She was so short and Jonathan so tall that her mouth was level with Jonathan's ear. Her voice was soft and gentle. "It is not what you said that was wrong; it's how you went about it."

Jonathan frowned. "What do you mean?"

"I mean if you continue to make outbursts, then people will not take you seriously. They will only look at you in an unfriendly light. Because of that, even if you are in the right, the majority of people will not listen."

Jonathan nodded and exclaimed, "I get that, but it just gets me so upset!"

"I know, but if not for your own cause, think about how your actions affect me and the class."

"I think I get it. By me acting out and you not punishing me, you either say acting out is okay or you're setting up a double standard when you punish someone else."

The teacher nodded, smiling, and moved back to the door. Opening it, she said for everyone else to hear, "Come on, Mr. Campbell, and let's finish this class."

Walking inside after her, Jonathan hurried to his desk, doing his best to ignore the snickers from much of the class as he sat down next to his friends. Trevor, who was sitting behind him, gave him a reassuring pat on the back and a smile when Jonathan turned to glance at him. It spoke volumes, more than him saying anything.

Cory, in front of Jonathan, turned in his seat and whispered, "Why are you such a glutton for punishment? You're not Neal."

"I know. I just couldn't help it," answered Jonathan in a hushed voice. Cory rolled his eyes and turned to listen to Mrs. Miller as she started to talk about the assignment. Jonathan made an effort to tune back in.

"For this five-hundred-word essay, I want you to examine the historical context of the Declaration of Independence. I would like this back by next Monday." As she finished, the strident bell rang, and the bustle of activity began as ready-to-leave students made their way to the door. Jonathan and his friends were, as usual, the last to leave, having not gotten their things ready to go.

As Jonathan passed, Mrs. Miller smiled at him, asking, "Jonathan, for this assignment, would you like to go outside the box?"

He frowned at her but nodded, unsure. His friends looked back to him as they went through the door.

"We'll wait for you, man," said Trevor, giving Jonathan a supportive smile.

"Yeah, but hurry," added Cory.

Mrs. Miller grinned, showing very white teeth against her red lips. Jonathan, in spite of the fact that it was inappropriate, had a twinge of longing from his navel region.

"Jonathan, since you're so interested in the effect things have on the Native Americans, I thought you might find it interesting to write about how the Declaration of Independence was understood by them. One way you could look at this is through them supporting the British in the Revolutionary War."

Jonathan grinned and said, "I'd love to. Thank you so much," then urged himself to move to the door and not to be weird and hug her. She waved a hand at him, and Jonathan exited into the hallway.

CHAPTER 5

Their next and last class was environmental science, taught by Mr. Johnson. He was a tall, bald African American man in his early fifties, with a bushy graying beard, which he was apparently quite proud of from the way he stroked it when thinking. Jonathan and his friends strategically sat in the back so Brandon, one of the bullies from lunch, couldn't throw pieces of paper at the back of their heads.

"So, did you get into trouble?" asked Cory seriously.

"No," Jonathan answered, then told his friends what had transpired both outside in the hall and after class.

"She's such a great teacher," remarked Trevor, opening his book and turning to the required page of the day's lesson.

Jonathan agreed. Instead of punishing him, she had told him how to better himself while allowing him to pursue something he was passionate to learn about. Jonathan opened to the page, as well, to find a stereotypical picture of a cave and bats. He groaned loudly enough for his friends to hear him. Jonathan liked both things, but with so many caves and bats around Hannibal, the subject was so mundane it sometimes became dull to learn the same things about it repeatedly.

"I know. I mean, caves are Hannibal's bread and butter. Why do we need to learn about something everyone should know about?" said

Cory a little too loudly.

"Because just because you know something, it doesn't mean others do; also, if you actually listen, you might learn something new, too," said Mr. Johnson in his deep baritone.

Cory blushed as many students looked at him and some snickered. However, others seemed to share Cory and Jonathan's feelings on the subject.

Mr. Johnson went on less sternly with his eyes on Neal, "Plus, like myself, some people like bats and caves." Indeed, Neal was vibrating in anticipation so hard it was a wonder he wasn't rattling the screws out of his chair.

Neal was also a nerd, but he could be annoying to Jonathan and Cory. He was just too weird. Trevor, though, went out of his way to stand up for Neal and even spend time with him outside of school. Neal was short and pudgy with the stereotypical thick glasses. His eyes were pale blue and always wary when you talked to him, like you were going to try to pull something on him. His blonde hair was his most noticeable feature. It was thick and so curly that no comb in the world could tame it.

Brandon chuckled darkly to himself at Neal's excitement. Brandon was even taller than Jonathan's six-foot-two frame. However, whereas Jonathan was skinny, Brandon had muscle stacked on top of muscle. His dark hair was cut short, and his dark-brown eyes looked like muddy pits. Trevor, although he often lost in his attempts to stand up for people, was unafraid of the large individual. Indeed, he seemed to enjoy the challenge.

"So, who here knows what bats we have in our caves around Hannibal?" asked Mr. Johnson. Neal's hand positively shot into the air. Mr. Johnson checked over the room to see if anyone else would raise their hand. Jonathan had learned his lesson in history, still kicking himself for his outburst, and did not raise his hand despite knowing the answer. Finally, after Trevor kicked him, Cory put his hand up, and Mr. Johnson pointed to him.

Neal wilted at missing out on what to him must have felt like the chance of a lifetime.

"Well, there are the little brown bats, the big brown bats, and the Indiana bats inside Sodalis Nature Preserve," said Cory in a bored voice.

"That's some of them. Perhaps Neal can tell us the rest," said Mr. Johnson, turning to grin expectantly at the eager boy. Cory looked flummoxed, but Neal bounded to his feet and said in a rush like an auctioneer, "There's the hoary bat, southern myotis, Rafinesque's big-eared bat, eastern small-footed bat, the Seminole bat, the gray bat or gray myotis, Eastern red bat, silver-haired bat, the Townsend's big-eared bat, the evening bat, the tricolored bat, and the northern long-eared myotis. And lastly, there are three free-tailed bats: the Brazilian free-tailed bat, the Mexican free-tailed bat, and the big free-tailed bat."

"That sounds right to me. Excellent job, Neal," said Mr. Johnson.

"Good job," whispered Trevor. When Neal turned, the friends all gave Neal thumbs up. He grinned so wildly that just then, Jonathan understood why Trevor was so nice to Neal.

Then, Brandon raised his hand, and Mr. Johnson hesitantly beckoned to him to add whatever he wanted to say. Brandon stood up, which was a statement in itself, with a dorky smile on his stupid face. "I think they forgot the big-eared, curly-haired nerd."

He laughed so hard as he flopped down in his chair again. For some reason, the other teens laughed as well, even though there was absolutely nothing funny about it. After a moment, Neal rushed from the room. Mr. Johnson sighed and raised one hand to silence the classroom. He went to his desk and called someone on the phone.

"I swear, one of these days I'll get even for all the kids who get picked on," said Trevor.

"Never mind him. Statistics show most people like that will end up at dead-end jobs, making minimum wage," consoled Cory.

"He's right. I bet those bullies won't even make it through high school."

Trevor gave a small, hopeful smile. Then, Mr. Johnson put down the phone, and the three friends looked at him expectantly. "Brandon, Principal O'Neal is expecting you."

"Yeah, whatever," said Brandon, getting up, sauntering over, and pushing open the classroom door. Jonathan could have sworn he saw Brandon laughing again as he put up a middle finger at the door closing behind him.

Mr. Johnson sighed, "Trevor, would you mind going to the counselor's office to help Neal?"

Trevor nodded, saying to his friends, "I'll meet you guys outside in a few minutes." They nodded to him, and Trevor hurried from the room.

The rest of the class went on without incident except for Jonathan continually nagging Cory about his incorrect answer. Finally, he exploded, "I was just trying to give Neal a chance!" Then, finally, the bell rang.

Outside the school, Jonathan hurried over to his friends, who were standing in their usual meeting place near the track. They gave Jonathan a high five and jumped as a car roared by them, horn blaring. Jonathan made to give the car the universal sign, but his friends pulled him away.

"Come on; ignore them," said Trevor, giving the car an anxious look to see its driver and passengers hadn't stopped to pester them.

"All right," Jonathan said, hiking up his backpack.

"Do you think we can grab a soda from your folks' place on the way?" asked Cory hopefully. It was a hot August day, and Jonathan's parents owned a curiosity shop on Main Street, so they usually could get sodas there. Jonathan nodded, trying to think of what he would tell his parents they were doing.

Trevor, seeing the look on Jonathan's face, seemed to read his mind, saying, "It'll be all right. Just tell them we are headed toward the lighthouse."

Jonathan nodded again, forcing a smile onto his face. He hated lying to his parents, but this was his chance to see if he could discover something new. "Our future would be made for us if it is a new species or something. Think about it, guys," said Jonathan, trying to get his mind off being untruthful to his parents.

"The statistical possibility of that is very slim. It could just be a black bear that was sick or had a few screws loose," Cory cautioned automatically.

"I would find it hard to believe a black bear with such issues would get this far north without people knowing," said Trevor.

Jonathan thought about that. Years earlier, in the nineteen fifties and sixties, Arkansas had succeeded at reintroducing black bears into the state. However, the bears had resolutely made their way north into Missouri as territory became more scarce. Many of them became dependent on humans for their food. So, some bears began raiding trash cans and even breaking into houses. Still, Jonathan was on Trevor's side. If there was such a bear, wouldn't it have been found already?

"I'm with Trevor. You're only saying that because you're scared of that movie that was made about the bear that ate all that cocaine in Georgia," said Jonathan.

"Am not," whined Cory.

Wanting to change the subject, Trevor pointed out some tourists walking around the Mark Twain Museum. One tourist wore a shirt that said *I dig caves*.

"Always the same," commented Trevor. "They all look at Twain's beginning and things of his childhood. I would be more interested in his life on the river boat or during his book tours. Hell, it must have been such a huge thing with his daughter having her epilepsy problems."

Trevor loved Mark Twain. Twain was a major reason people came to Hannibal. Growing up as a kid there, however, the same stories got old. They saw only a piece of the great man who well deserved to be remembered for his gifts to mankind. Trevor hated that much of Twain's work resided on banned-book lists where they stayed, never to be read by many kids and teens. Trevor had once said, "Twain's books are a historical snapshot of the past. If we don't learn from it, we are doomed to repeat it. Plus, you read books for their accuracy, not to skate around the truth of how things were."

"Hey, don't forget the ferryboat museum," chided Jonathan, trying to break his friend's dark thoughts. The ferryboat museum was a great snapshot of one of Twain's loves.

"Yeah, I suppose," said Trevor.

"We'd better step on it, guys," Cory said. "Do you think your parents fixed that fridge yet, Jonathan?"

"I hope so. I hate warm soda," answered Jonathan, and they all laughed, including Trevor.

The boys crossed Center Street and entered Jonathan's parents' store. There was the familiar musty odor of antiques mixed with the overwhelming smell of herbs—everything from cooking herbs to medicinal ones that were often used in Native American medicine.

Jonathan's mother greeted the boys with a warm smile and a hug just for her son. Her sable hair was plaited in a long braid, which she wore over her shoulder.

"And what are you boys up to on this hot August day?" she asked lovingly.

"Oh, you know us, just raising hell with a couple sodas, if we could get some please," asked Cory with a devilish smile. Jonathan's mom laughed and waved them over to the fridge.

"Thank you, Mrs. Campbell," said Trevor dutifully.

"We're just gonna go up to see the bats come out. Is it okay if the guys spend the night?" asked Jonathan.

His mother's hazel eyes clouded with concern, but then she forced a smile. "You boys just be safe and stick together. And remember, we are having Imo's tonight at seven."

"Thanks, Mom," said Jonathan, giving his mother another hug.

"Imo's is the best pizza," said Cory, pumping a fist in the air. The boys laughed, and the three made their way to the door, thanking Jonathan's mom on their way out.

Cory shouted over his shoulder, "Don't worry, Mrs. C—I'll keep your Johnny boy safe."

They heard Jonathan's mom laugh as Jonathan gave a halfhearted swing at Cory, which Cory dodged good-naturedly. Trevor grabbed Jonathan's arm as he toppled over, tripping on an eroded brick. Together, they headed towards Bear Creek, walking out onto Main Street and taking in the old building with familiar eyes. Nothing jumped out at Jonathan as unusual. Soon, they reached Bear Creek and hurried onto the well-made path that twisted and turned through the woods.

CHAPTER 6

George Cummings hurried through the woods of Sodalis Preserve the best his bad leg would let him. *Everything has hurt ever since 'Nam. I need my damn oxy. But the damn pigs keep running me off my bench. A man's got to get his sleep*, thought George, angrily pushing aside branches.

"If the damn government took care of their own, they'd give me my oxy," he said loudly. Then he stopped, and he could hear those damn pigs coming after him. "Why's it such a big deal? I always sleep on the benches. I ain't bugging no one," he hissed.

George had fought for his country in Vietnam and had gotten shrapnel in his leg. When he got home, he had expected to be treated like a war hero; instead, as many had been, he was ridiculed for his actions. Even his own family had turned their backs on him. And Susan, who he had hoped to marry, had married another guy, a rich one, and moved out to L.A.

Now that those pigs were after him, he had to get out of there or find a place to hide. He couldn't afford to go back to jail. Just a few years earlier, he had gotten arrested for drug possession. How did the government expect him to pay for his jail time when he had no money? George pushed a pine branch aside, spraying needles everywhere when he let the limb go. Rubbing his hand that was now sticky with sap, George looked around.

He nearly leapt for joy at what he saw. The many entrances to Sodalis' caves were all barricaded against any people trying to get in, but they had gaps to allow the bats, which made the caves their home, to get in and out. Here, however, someone had removed the bars, probably with a saw. The shiny and well-constructed bars were red with what George thought must be rough. He couldn't see any sign of the person who had done this. Also, this entrance was so little known and hidden by bushes that he could use this to his advantage.

"Government's cutting corners all over, even out here. Well, a cave would be better than most places I've slept. At least there is a God." With that, George crawled inside.

The cave floor was rocky but dry. George, his luck turning for once, figured all he needed now was some food. Curious about what he would find, George walked deeper into the cave. As one would expect, it was soon too dark to see. George, with his bad leg, nearly tripped over something that crunched, and he fell against the cave wall.

He groaned in pain as he pulled himself upright, his leg throbbing. Muttering profanities, he made to keep going. He froze as he heard footsteps from the darkness. George was scared, but as he thought about it, what did he have to be scared of? He knew all the other homeless around Hannibal.

"Who's there? I didn't know anyone had claimed this cave. I can go to another part of it. I'm sure it's a big cave."

It watched the old man limping along with one hand to the wall of the cave. The only reason the man was not dead already and just meat to be consumed was because it had been sleeping and was now taken aback by the stupidity of this old guy. It had been almost thirty years since a lone human had set foot in the caves. Other people had entered, but they had been in large groups, looking at flying rodents. But, it was awake now.

The weird meat with guns had let it out. And they had given it something that made it feel . . . exhilarated.

However, the meat before him would still die; there was no reason to rush as the man came closer and closer. An idea stuck that would hasten the man's demise. In a croaky, weak voice, it said, "Help me, please." The man, as planned, hurried forward. *Stupid meat. Meat is always stupid*, it thought. Then the man, groping in a pocket, pulled out a lighter and flicked it.

The despised heat was horrible, and in hatred and fear, it leapt forward. The man, finally seeing the nightmare before him, froze, and his bad leg buckled under him. Sucking in breath to scream, with his eyes wide, the old man desperately waved the flame at it. Quick as a bolt of lightning, it knocked the meat's hand aside and tore out the meat's throat.

The meat gurgled and lay back, motionless, as the creature bent over its surprise meal. Hardly had it taken what was wanted than there were more sounds from outside the cave. These voices were young and a little way off. However, now that it was awake, of course it was always hungry.

CHAPTER 7

The banks of Bear Creek were deserted. "It's weird seeing no one here— and kind of creepy, don't you think, Jonathan?" said Trevor, a little nervously. As he spoke, a twig or stick snapped in the woods, making all three boys whip around.

Cory laughed and said in a slightly high voice, "Naw, you're just silly. It's just a creek, not the Mall of America."

But Jonathan thought he knew what Trevor meant as the three walked on the well-paved path. Normally, the scenic creek had at least a handful of people, like kids playing at the creek's edge or looking for crawdads, or adults taking in nature with the calming sounds of the babbling water. However, now all those traits that made the area scenic suddenly made the boys feel like they were far from home and all alone.

"So, if it's a person that killed those people, we really are getting in over our heads," said Trevor, carrying on a conversation from earlier.

Jonathan looked at his friend, whose face was pale and whose eyes were jumping around like crickets. "I doubt it. If the murderer were a person, I don't think they would be so hush hush about it being a human," said Jonathan bracingly.

He continued, excitement raising his voice's pitch, "What if we actually find something that no one else knows about? Think about it: a new discovery and our names etched into history."

"I'm just saying that statistical probability—" answered Cory, but he broke off as another twig broke in the underbrush. They all froze. Jonathan even found himself holding his breath with trepidation and fear. Where had all the bluster and excitement of discovery gone?

Some brave adventurers we are, thought Jonathan bitterly.

Then a shrub shook, and a gray squirrel jumped out onto the river rocks. The three boys looked at each other and broke out into laughter. They laughed so hard the squirrel leapt back into the woods. Walking on, Jonathan pounded Cory on his back because he had started to cough from his laughter.

The monster watched the boys hungrily, thirsty for their blood. However, the bright sun hurt, so it watched them go. Then, as quiet as a shadow and keeping to the shade, it began to follow to see if it would have its chance to gorge itself again. It leapt up a tree and then jumped from one to another faster than any squirrel and as silent as a mosquito. It stored the information it had learned for later. Now it knew one of the meat's names was Jonathan, and Jonathan was dangerous.

Coming around a turn in the creek, Jonathan grabbed the two other boys by the back of their shirt collars. Trevor turned, exclaiming, "What the—" but Jonathan's face was serious with a finger to his lips. Then Trevor motioned them over to a large stump at the edge of the woods and quickly ducked behind it. Jonathan was next, with Cory following, a bemused expression on his face.

Trevor whispered in Jonathan's ear, "What's up?"

"Yeah, where's the well, Lassie?" joked Cory.

Jonathan jostled him with a shoulder, but they both grinned before Jonathan whispered, annoyed, "Just listen! You two are deaf."

Cory fell silent and listened. After a moment, they all heard it and had to admit Trevor and Cory must be deaf. Further down the creek, maybe fifteen feet away, bushes were rustling, and then a man was swearing under his breath.

"I don't see him anywhere," said a loud, nasally voice.

Then a young man stepped out onto the rocks of the beach and sneezed forcefully. He wore a police officer's uniform, and his nose and eyes were red. "Come on, Sheriff. He ditched us. And as long as he ain't on the scene, what's the big deal?" asked the officer mournfully. Then he sniffed and rubbed his red nose with the back of his hand.

Sheriff Roland stomped on the beach, his face red under his wide-brimmed tan hat. The sheriff glared at the young officer, saying, "It's not that he's left the area; it's that he came onto a crime scene and was asked multiple times to leave the area. Disturbing an ongoing crime scene is against the law. It was reported to me several times. It wasn't until we showed up that he ran off."

"Oh, come on. It's hot out here, sir," whined the officer.

Sheriff Roland grabbed the officer by his collar and got in his face, growling, "If you want to move up the ranks, you'll learn the ways. When you let things slide on your watch, you are allowing crime to flourish!"

The officer stepped back, shaking slightly, "Y-yes, sir," he sputtered.

Sheriff Roland stepped away, saying, "Plus, we need to keep our streets clean of his type. Don't need people like him around, especially during an election year."

"Yes, sir," said the officer again, looking down at his shoes. Then he continued, "It's just that we should be giving a more detailed report. Put people on alert for some type of animal—right, Sheriff?"

The sheriff's red face paled, and he said soberly, "Never seen anything like that. And it ain't no animal I've ever seen do what happened to those poor kids."

The officer nodded, and he seemed hopeful. However, the sheriff drew in a breath and said, "But, no reason to put out too much information. Ain't no reason to scare people. Chances are whatever did this already left the area." The officer's shoulders seemed to slump. "Just tell anyone that asks that it was likely an animal, but that we haven't seen any signs that it's still in the area. That's close enough to the truth," said Sheriff Roland.

The sheriff turned to head back to where the two had come from. The officer hurried to follow. As the two passed into the woods, Jonathan heard the sheriff say, "Let me know if that old man shows up. Also, keep an eye out for that fellow in the fedora. He's been asking questions around town. People been telling me he's been bugging them about the history of the mine."

"I'll keep an eye out, sir," answered the officer's voice, which grew fainter as the two hurried back to what must be the crime scene.

The whole time the two had been speaking, Jonathan felt a freezing chill come over him. Looking down at his arms, he saw goosebumps covering them. Trevor nudged him and whispered, "Let's get the hell out of here."

Jonathan nodded his agreement, and Cory answered in a quiet voice, "Yeah, my parents would kill me if I got in trouble with the cops." With that, the three hurried away, back towards Market Street.

Perplexed, it watched the meat go. A feeling kept coming over it that it must kill the meat named Jonathan. It had always killed to try to satiate its constant hunger, but some part of the creature screamed at itself that Jonathan must die. Not for food, but because Jonathan was dangerous to it. It was beyond its understanding; Jonathan wasn't threatening it. Still, it couldn't let go of the feeling of danger around Jonathan.

Some part of it rebelled, and so it whispered Jonathan's name just to see its prey squirm like usual. However, as Jonathan looked over his shoulder, it was the creature that flinched as the boy's brown eyes passed over a tree near to where it hid. Once Jonathan was out of sight, it hurried back home to the safety of the cold, dark cave.

CHAPTER 8

The three friends reached the familiar sights and sounds of Collier Street. A few cars rumbled by, the smell of their exhaust instantly killing the fresh smell of Bear Creek. They walked along and soon came to Main Street. Bells here and there tinkled as people of all ages hurried in and out of stores, the busiest store being, of course, the candy store.

Jonathan pointed out their bullies from lunch skulking around Becky's Old Fashioned Ice Cream, trying to chat up some girls in overly short skirts. "Those guys are absolute Neanderthals," stated Cory, making his friends laugh quietly as they hurried by on the opposite side of the street. They turned left on Center Street, passing The Brick Oven, a popular pizza restaurant.

Then Jonathan saw something coming out of his parents' shop that made him pause. Just passing the pawn shop called Rags to Riches was a short man with a trim, light-brown beard. In spite of the heat, he wore a white dress shirt and a purple vest. His black pants matched his shiny black shoes perfectly. To complete his outfit, he quickly put on a black fedora and, of course, used a well-polished cane with what looked like a gold handle, though Jonathan couldn't see the handle's shape.

"Do you think that's the guy the officers meant?" asked Jonathan.

"Must be; he sure does stick out," added Trevor.

Indeed, as the short man walked away from them, they could see people turning to gape at him. To the boys, he looked like he belonged on Wall Street or in Congress, not here in Hannibal, Missouri.

"What do you think he would want with your parents?" asked Cory, his voice skeptical, as though he couldn't believe this man could want anything to do with Jonathan's parents.

"I don't know, but I'll try to ask my parents about it tonight," answered Jonathan, choosing to ignore Cory's tone. He could be a bit rude, but he usually didn't mean anything by it. Trevor faced Jonathan with a knowing look and gave him a pat on the back.

Pushing open the door, the group was greeted by Jonathan's father, who wore an expression of concern and thoughtfulness. But his face changed upon seeing the boys as he smiled widely. Adam Campbell had short brown hair the same shade as Jonathan's. Beneath his thin eyebrows, his brown eyes always seemed to twinkle with amusement. Mr. Campbell was tall and skinny like Jonathan, with high cheekbones and not a hint of stubble on his face.

"Boys, good to see you! I heard we were doing Imo's tonight. I hope you are ready," said Mr. Campbell in his deep, cheerful voice.

"Hi, Dad. You know we kids have bottomless stomachs. I hope you have the dough for it."

Mr. Campbell's face fell comically, then he laughed. "I'm sure we have enough to get a few crumbs," he quipped. Jonathan, his father, and Trevor laughed.

Cory threw his hands up in the "aww, heck no—I am not dealing with dad puns this early in the evening" kind of way.

"Oh, come on. There's no reason to get such a rise out of Cory," said Jonathan. The three comedic savants roared with laughter as Cory stormed over to the fridge. He pulled open the door forcefully, grabbed a root beer, and popped the top off the bottle with a bottle opener that hung on the fridge's handle.

Stepping outside with his own root beer in hand, Jonathan blew the fog that always flowed out of the bottle once the cap popped. He took a long drink, smacking his lips in delight at the creamy smoothness of the beverage. His eyes were closed, and he felt relaxed now. He inhaled deeply through his nose, breathing in the world around him.

The smell of the city was present. Exhaust fumes from cars dominated, but the boys also detected the smell of barbeque and fried fish. Then the wind shifted, bringing a distant hint of something fresh and earthy. Jonathan's eyes automatically turned to the source he knew it would be: the great Mississippi River. He could see the inexorable brown water flowing past in the distance.

Jonathan watched the water flowing by. People had lived by the Mississippi's banks since the distant past. Everyone knew about the Cahokia who had lived and thrived around the area. The mounds they had made were well known. Jonathan had been to the museum of the Cahokia mounds the year before, and they had been impressive to say the least. St. Louis was even known as Mound City by some because of all the mounds scattered around the area.

"What would the world be like without the muddy Mississippi," mused Jonathan aloud.

A sarcastic thought answered in his mind, *Well, you wouldn't have horrible floods like the food of 1993.* While that was true, it ignored what the river provided. Without it, Missouri's farms would not be so fertile, as the river brought much-needed nutrients. The river also made the caves that had been used to build industry and the very buildings that made St. Louis.

Heck, without the river, goods being transported up and down the waterway would not be possible. It made the people, as well. One didn't have to look further than Mark Twain, whose very pseudonym referenced measuring the river depth when boating on the river. "The world would be far less rich without the river," Jonathan said, voicing his thought aloud.

"You got that right," said Trevor from behind Jonathan, making him jump.

Trevor let out a chuckle and went on, "Hannibal wouldn't be here if the river had not made the caves. Weren't the Sodalis Caves originally one of the cave systems that were heavily mined?"

Jonathan nodded. "Yeah, I think they were used to mine cement."

"So what made them stop? It wasn't just the bats being there, was it?" asked Trevor.

"I don't know," Jonathan answered, his mind jumping into overdrive. "Could there be something else behind them having gates at the entrances? What if they are not only trying to keep people out but also something in?"

Trevor gave him a skeptical look and answered, "I don't know about that. Don't you think we would have heard about something like that?"

Jonathan blushed but still felt confident he could be on to a real hometown conspiracy. It was exciting, but for now, he would let it go, at least until he was at home with his computer.

The door to the store was pushed jerkily open, and Cory whined, "You guys can't just leave me in this hell."

Jonathan and Trevor laughed, and they heard Mr. Campbell say, "Aw, come on, Cory. Don't get flaky with me."

"Oh my God, that is the worst one yet," answered Cory, going back inside as Jonathan and Trevor followed.

"That was pretty forced, Dad," said Jonathan, trying not to laugh more at Cory's look of absolute suffering.

Mr. Campbell just laughed, and Mrs. Campbell pushed through the swinging door from the back room. She smiled at them all warmly, her dimples showing. "Glad you boys are here. I just finished ordering supplies," she said. She looked hard at them and gave her husband an overly stern gaze after seeing Cory's expression. "Have you been torturing these boys again?" They laughed as Mr. Campbell's face fell comically and Cory gave a fake sniff of tears.

She slapped her palms together, saying, "Well then, let's get the pizza."

"Don't forget the fried ravioli," exclaimed Cory in mock horror as they all walked out to the family van.

"How could we ever forget that?" mocked Jonathan. Though, if he was truthful, the fried ravioli was to die for.

CHAPTER 9

At six thirty-five, they reached Jonathan's house. He felt the day's tension release at the sight of the small two-story house. It was old and shabby, like many of the other houses on the block. However, there was something at the sight of his home's fading blue paint that just felt right.

As the group piled out and walked to the front door, Jonathan carried the three pizzas, the boxes warm in his hands. His dad pulled the white door open with a slight creak that was as familiar as the sight of himself in a mirror. Cory and Trevor hurried after Jonathan, Cory with a large box that held the toasted ravioli and Trevor with three two-liter bottles of Coca-Cola. Jonathan's mother pulled up the rear, carrying a large plastic bowl of salad.

They set the boxes down on the kitchen table, a large, heavy wooden piece that had been passed down from Jonathan's grandparents on his mother's side. Much of the furniture and other odds and ends in their home had been passed down in the family. Here and there, one could see their family's Native American roots. A necklace of bright-colored beads hung from one shelf of the overfilled bookcase. A tomahawk lay innocently on a shelf next to an old, faded picture of Mr. Campbell's father.

He, unlike Jonathan's father, was the spitting image of what someone would call a Native American, although he wore 'normal' clothes, possibly trying to blend in. Not too long ago, Native Americans were seen as something to be stepped on. So, many people chose to try to do just what Jonathan's grandfather had likely done—blend in. However, in doing so they left behind their identity, and Jonathan could understand why the tribes that still existed today found it hard to accept those who had once turned their back on their own people.

As always, Jonathan eyed these reminders of the past with awe and a bit shamefully, as though he was doing something wrong. Lastly, he looked at what he knew must be a true Native American artifact. It was a large knife that sat on top of the bookshelf as though it was his father's pride and joy, which Jonathan thought it might be. The handle was made of antler. The sheath was well-worn leather covered in animal symbols. The blade itself was dark and weathered, with a single sharp edge.

The one time Jonathan had gotten a look at it was burned into his memory, not just because he had been awed by the weapon and the history it must hold, but also, because his father had been irate at what he had called "sneaking around and stealing what wasn't yet his." Mr. Campbell wasn't a stern man—far from it—but in this case, he had flown into such a terrible mood.

Jonathan caught his father looking at him, but to Jonathan's consternation, his face appeared thoughtful. Grabbing a paper plate, Jonathan began to pile it with the cardboard-thin pizza squares. He grabbed plenty of the plain cheese and the deluxe pizza and a couple slices of the meat lover's. Then, he realized he had no space on his plate for his toasted ravioli. Shrugging to himself, he placed a few ravioli on top of his pizza for an appetizer.

His mom laughed, saying, "Maybe we should have gotten six pizzas instead of just three."

"Don't you know, honey, that junk food calories are how growing teens get big and strong?" quipped his dad. Jonathan flushed, seeing that the three boys had taken the majority of the three pizzas.

"We can't save Princess Zelda without energy," stated Cory.

The group loved the *Legend of Zelda* games. Since *Tears of the Kingdom* had come out, the group had taken on the task of beating every Zelda game. Currently, they were on *Majora's Mask*.

"I am amazed at you, Cory. You're such a stickler for stating facts, but you just stated a falsehood," said Trevor with a smile on his face. Nonplussed, Cory quirked an eyebrow at Trevor, who glanced at Jonathan as if to say, "You get it, right?"

Jonathan thought for a second, then he gave a quick laugh. "I get it. Good one, Trevor."

Trevor bowed, chuckling to himself. Cory looked at the others blankly. In the background of this, Jonathan heard the living room TV turn on as his parents sat down to hear the day's news. Jonathan gestured for his friends to follow him as they made their way to the stairs that led to his room.

"He means how can you be saving Princess Zelda at all when she isn't even a main character in *Majora's Mask*?" said Jonathan.

Jonathan waved to his parents as he and his friends began to ascend the stairs. Stoked by his insightful victory, Cory continued, "*Majora's Mask* doesn't even take place in Hyrule; it takes place in Termina!"

Trevor blushed bright red. "Oh, you two, shut up. You know what I meant." Jonathan and Cory both smiled as they reached the landing and turned right, Jonathan pushing open his bedroom door.

His room was a paradise—as long as you were a nerd. Nintendo games and comics packed his bookshelf. The ceiling was slanted with the angle of the roof. Lining three walls of the room were posters dedicated to his loves, from the bigfoot poster depicting the cryptid's big, hairy legs in the foreground, a dark forest in the background, and the age-old words *The Truth is Out There,* to a poster of Moon Knight jumping from a tall building, his cape flowing and the enormous moon directly behind him.

Against one wall was the wardrobe, and next to it was a small dresser displaying several figurines used for *Dungeons and Dragons* and a mirror over it. Jonathan's twin bed was under the room's window that looked out over the town as it fell away towards the river. On the opposite side of the room were his desk and computer. The desk was cluttered with papers on his thoughts, a diary spread out like an octopus, and drawings he had made from his imagination. Cryptids, of course, featured in most of his drawings.

Next to the desk, on a small, wobbly table, sat Jonathan's TV. Under the desk were his Super Nintendo, N64, Wii, and Switch. Coming into the room, the three boys went to their usual spots. Cory grabbed the fold-out surround-sound chair and placed it in front of the TV. Trevor plopped down in front of the computer and powered it on, getting ready to open a tab for a game walkthrough. Moving to sit on his bed, Jonathan watched his friends for a minute. It never seemed odd to him that their seating positions were just natural, like closing the refrigerator door when you were done with it. Exhaling, he fell back lazily onto his bed, his long legs hanging off the side.

Pulling out his phone, Jonathan began to cruise the net as he quickly demolished his toasted ravioli. In the background, the TV turned on, and soon the familiar sounds of the games played. Trevor spoke up between bites of his cheese pizza. "I believe we had just finished the Goron level? Do we want to upgrade our sword before we leave the area?"

"I think we should get the sword. It makes the game so much easier," stated Jonathan as he opened his notes in his phone to form a list of possible cryptid culprits.

"Yeah, but doesn't that mean having to do the Goron race for the ore to make the sword?" whined Cory as he cashed in his rupees with the banker in Clock Town. That way his rupees didn't run back to zero when he played the Song of Time to warp time back to the first day.

"Yes, that's right," said Jonathan, grinning as he took his first bite of cheese pizza. The provel cheese, as always, tasted amazing. Running a search for *cryptids of the Midwest*, he came up with two that were possible: the Momo monster and the Ozark howler.

He quickly wrote the two names down, both of which he knew a good bit about because they were local to Missouri. He heard Cory play the Song of Time while muttering to himself as he ate a square of pizza in two big bites. Trevor typed away on the computer.

"What are you looking up, Trevor?" asked Jonathan.

Without looking over, Trevor replied, "Looking up if there are any missing or dead animals in the area that could be attributed to our attacker."

Jonathan smiled, and he was glad Trevor was there to think of things he had not. "Great idea. That could help us determine how long it's been here and how much it needs to eat."

"This stupid Dodongo will not die," exclaimed Cory.

Jonathan looked up in time to see Cory's character attempt to backflip over the Dodongo's tail as the overly large lizard spun. Cory wasn't fast enough, and the *Game Over* screen came up. Jonathan tried not to chuckle at Cory taking angry bites of his pieces of meat-lover's pizza.

Trevor cleared his throat, and Cory gave him an annoyed look. However, he ignored Cory and said, "You know, I've heard that Shigeru Miyamoto came up with *The Legend of Zelda* because he wanted to instill the feelings of discovery and wonder that he felt when adventuring in the countryside when he was young."

"And what does that have to do with the price of tea in China?" answered Cory heatedly.

Jonathan knew what Trevor meant, though. "I agree. It's fitting to be playing such a game when we ourselves are trying to solve a mystery."

"Okay, you two Scooby-Doo fans can get up to all the hijinks you want to. Just make sure you let me beat this stupid side quest!" It was an understatement to say that Cory did not like to lose at games.

"Why are you trying to kill that Dodongo, anyway?" asked Jonathan.

"Because he breathed fire on me when I tried to go down the hole in the ground near him," answered Cory with forced calm in his voice.

Jonathan smiled at Trevor and winked. Trevor smiled back, stifling his own humor as he spun his chair to turn back to the computer.

Jonathan typed a new search: *cryptids that eat people*. The first name he saw made him pause, a tingle of fear running down his spine. The name of the creature was the wendigo.

CHAPTER 10

A second shiver ran down Jonathan's back, and he drew up his feet so he was nearly fetal. The wendigo was a nightmare from the Ojibwe people's past. It was known in Jonathan's mind as a true monster. In Ojibwe legend, the wendigo was the personification of winter. During times of starvation, the spirit of the wendigo would take you over. Once this was done, the wendigo would push you to cannibalism.

People that were said to have been taken over by the spirit would do terrible acts. One of these cases could have been the infamous Donner Party. The chiefs and shaman of the Ojibwe tribe would track down those who were turning into one of these creatures. And there was a well-known public case where a shaman named Jack Fiddler claimed to have killed fourteen wendigo.

However, Fiddler was arrested when he killed a woman who he said was turning into a wendigo. Whether his claim was true or not, the court in question did not care, nor did they believe or even try to understand the wendigo legend. Fiddler took his own life in 1907 after being convicted of the woman's murder. For the people of the Ojibwe and many other Algonquin cultures, the wendigo was a real threat.

Like his ancestors, Jonathan believed the legends. Those who turned into the wendigo became very tall and emaciated. They were said to be fast and strong. The wendigo, for many, was considered the North American version of the vampire.

Being the embodiment of greed and cannibalism, the wendigo was never satiated. Bloodthirsty but supremely intelligent, they were the hunters of man . . . and sometimes beast. Nothing could be worse than to be eaten by something that once called itself human. There was just something inherently wrong in one human eating another, which must be why it was believed the act of cannibalism changed you.

Jonathan, with his eyes closed, could see the image of a wendigo in his head: over seven feet tall with pure-white skin pulled taught over an emaciated frame. Its hands were tipped with nails that could tear you apart. The teeth were stained red and sharp as daggers. However, worst of all were the green eyes exuding greed, bloodlust, hate, and death. They drew you in, making you helpless to run or fight. You could only die.

Heedless to Jonathan's churning fears, Cory complained loudly, "This game is such a fever dream when you think about it."

"I think that's the point," chortled Trevor. Then, there was the groan and squeak of the computer chair as he turned to look at Jonathan. "You okay, man?"

"Yeah, just got a chill," answered Jonathan, pulling the cover over himself and trying to look relaxed.

Trevor didn't look at all convinced, but he asked, "Did you find any likely culprits?"

Still unnerved, Jonathan answered, "The first thing that pops up on a search for cryptids that eat people is the wendigo." He said this with a plea in his voice, as though asking for information to invalidate his findings.

Trevor gave him a look of understanding and pity. "I don't think it would be that. With what you told me about the wendigo, there would be a lot more deaths in the area. Apart from the recent attack, the number of pets going missing has not been unusual."

Trevor's reasoning did make Jonathan feel a bit better. This information meant that they could narrow down their search to creatures that preferred humans as their main diet. Jonathan always thought of a wendigo as a voracious killer that ate anything and everything.

As if to add to this upward swing in Jonathan's mood, Cory stated, without taking his eyes off the screen, "Yeah, aren't those things supposed to be all about the winter? I mean, sure it gets cold here in the winter, but it's summer right now."

"That's true, but I don't think they are endemic to only arctic areas. I think it's more about the things winter is associated with." Though he argued the point with Cory, Jonathan was feeling even more relieved.

"Well," Cory said, "I still think old Frosty would not like this place in summer."

Trevor smiled at Jonathan. "Did you find any others?"

Jonathan looked down at his small list and answered, "There are two known cryptids in Missouri, the Momo monster and the Ozark howler."

Cory actually turned to Jonathan with a laugh and said, "Really, man? Both of those are nothing more than crazy, drunk rednecks that saw a bear or a coyote."

Jonathan put up a deprecating hand. "I'll give you that the Ozark howler is weak, that it's probably sightings of a mountain lion, and the howls are probably from some type of coyote group. However, what if the Momo monster is just another name for bigfoot?"

Cory rolled his eyes, and Trevor looked at the TV. In a deadpan voice, Trevor said, "You're about to lose your sword to the crow."

Cory cursed and turned back to the game, making his character do a bunch of front rolls to try to escape the pilfering bird. Jonathan snorted, and Cory threw him a middle finger as he continued his character's mad dash towards the edge of the map to a new area.

"So, you were talking about the Momo monster?" asked Trevor, turning back to the computer and typing a search for the creature.

Jonathan got up and pointed at the image on the screen. "You can see a lot of similarities between creatures such as the Momo monster, the swamp ape, bigfoot, and the yeti." Trevor nodded his agreement, and Jonathan felt like a professor teaching a class as he brought up images of all those creatures in new tabs to illustrate the commonalities.

"I see what you mean, but just come out and say where are you going with this, Jonathan," said Trevor.

"I think I know," piped up Cory, as if in class.

"Well, go ahead then, Cory," said Jonathan, adding a deeper register to his voice.

Cory paused the game and then turned fully to his friends. "Jonathan here believes as some do that these are sightings of the remnants of the Gigantopithecus."

Cory grinned as Jonathan said, still in his teacher's voice, "Give the boy a gold star! Isn't it a bit arrogant to think we are the only simian to thrive and be alive today?"

"Okay, but I thought most evidence found about these creatures was inconclusive," questioned Trevor, looking between his friends.

Cory and Jonathan both shook their heads. "The only evidence that has been found of Gigantopithecus is a jaw bone with teeth from somewhere in China," said Cory.

Jonathan added sadly, "Finding so little evidence of such creatures limits our understanding of them."

Trevor frowned. "So does the fact that there being so little evidence reduces the possibility of the creature living still."

Cory and Jonathan looked at each other and then together shrugged at Trevor while he pulled up their original search for *cryptids that eat people*. Cory and Jonathan both stepped up to stand on either side of Trevor's chair. While Trevor began to scroll down the page, Jonathan did his best to ignore the continued mentions of the wendigo.

"Are these three possible?" said Trevor, pointing out a list of three other cryptids: ghouls, Black Annis, and Blemmyes.

"What the heck is a Black Annis? Did someone just walk into a bathroom when another person was bending over for their underwear?" Cory quipped.

Jonathan gave a small chuckle at the low-hanging fruit and said, "It's pronounced *Ann – iss*," with a roll of his eyes.

Trevor gave Cory a scathing look as he clicked on the name, pulling up a link, and he began to read aloud. "'The Black Annis, sometimes also called Black Annie or Black Cat, is a bogeywoman that hails from Leicestershire, England.' It says she has blue skin and long nails. And she seems to love eating children."

"She sounds like a tale parents would tell their children. 'Eat all your veggies or the Black Annis will get you,'" said Cory in a silly, spooky voice.

Jonathan gave Cory a dirty look and argued, "The story of the Annis is well known enough to get itself a spot in the *Witcher* series." Cory gave him a "whatever" look and rolled his eyes.

"What about the other two?" asked Trevor in an overly large voice.

"I don't think it would be ghouls," Jonathan answered. "I know it says they eat people, but I always think of them as only being in graveyards. I just can't think of them ripping open a car to get at two in-shape teenagers."

"Yeah, the Black Annis has the same problem. Remember it said she went after younger kids," added Trevor. Jonathan nodded in agreement.

"So what about the Blemmyes? Weren't those creatures in *A Midsummer Night's Dream*?" asked Trevor.

Cory nodded and added, "If you were better at your history, you would know that both Herototis and Plemy the Elder talked about them."

"Be nice," said Jonathan, giving Cory a nudge. He suspected Cory hadn't gotten the names quite right, but he decided not to say anything because he wasn't sure.

Cory grinned at him, "I know, but he's such a hopeless romantic. Trevor needs to know more than just his Shakespeare."

Trevor said obliviously to both friends, "I don't think they would be our culprit. Multiple sites say that there was a real tribe of these Blemmyes. But they were probably just people with faces on their shields."

"Though I must point out that this tribe may have been copying some creature that was real; it is not unheard of," pointed out Jonathan.

"Okay, but even if it was a real creature, it would be a creature of Africa, not a creature of Hannibal, Missouri," said Cory, gesticulating.

Jonathan took a deep breath, and out of the corner of his eye, he caught sight of his favorite monster, a werewolf, on one of his posters. Jonathan grinned and leaned over Trevor and typed it into a search.

Before he had even finished typing out the word, Cory sighed, "Really, Jonathan—not a lycanthrope. We've been through this. They aren't real."

Trevor being Trevor began to scroll through the links, reading silently as Jonathan and Cory argued on a well-worn path.

The familiar argument proceeded as usual with Jonathan starting calmly, "No one in their right mind can overlook both the true historical evidence between the Beast of Gévaudan in the seventeen sixties, where over one hundred people died, and the execution of Peter Stumpf from Bedburg in fifteen eighty-nine. He literally admitted to killing those people and being a werewolf because of the belt the Devil gave him." By the end of this rebuttal, Jonathan was out of breath, and his face felt hot as Cory began to calmly pick apart his arguments.

"Both are historical; I'll give you that. But it is also historically accepted that the Beast of Gévaudan was done by a real wolf or hyena! And Stumpf was tortured. He would have said that the sky was green and purple if that had gotten them to stop. Anything he admitted to was a lie. And even if he thought he was a werewolf, the man was crazy! He could literally just be a person suffering from clinical lycanthropy."

Seeing his chance, Jonathan put in with a smile, "A clinical delusion which is not accepted by the board!"

Cory blushed deeply and spluttered, "It is more of an acceptable explanation than a person being a werewolf."

Jonathan smiled more widely and wagged a finger at Cory. "Ah, you forget about hypertrichosis, which is a completely real medical condition. Petrus Gonsalvus even became the inspiration for the story Beauty and the Beast."

"Wow, so you are condemning people who are suffering from a genetic disorder," answered Cory with a little smile.

Jonathan took in a breath, then expelled all the air from his lungs. He felt like a jerk.

Breaking in on the debate, Trevor asked out of nowhere, "What about the Beast of Bray Road?"

Cory threw his hands in the air and walked over to the bed. "Great. Now you have Trevor as a convert to your lunacy."

"I'm not going to point out how that word lunacy fits so well with our topic. But to answer your question, as you can see on this page you pulled up, that happened in Elkhorn, Wisconsin. Sightings go from nineteen thirty-six all the way up to twenty twenty. There have even been sightings of what some think is a family group."

In a low voice, Cory said, "I have to point out that there have been no human killings by the Beast of Bray Road."

Jonathan nodded, "That's true, but people have been attacked both in their cars and on foot. Also, livestock and deer were found mutilated."

Cory moved back to the computer, leaning over to click on the tab of *animals missing* posts. "Yeah, but here we've not seen animal mutilations with the attacks in our area, at least none I see here." He glanced at Jonathan with a questioning look then began to pace, apparently deep in thought.

Jonathan felt tired now. "You're right, but what else could it be?

I mean Amanda and Chris were in great shape, and it literally tore them out of their car." Suddenly, in spite of himself, he felt wetness at the corners of his eyes.

What was going on here? They were both bullies; he didn't even like either of them. A tear rolled unbidden down his cheek. Jonathan hurriedly wiped it away and looked at Trevor, whose eyes were wet, too. Trevor got up and put a comforting hand on Jonathan's back. Why was this happening? He felt like such a wimp.

Cory stopped pacing and looked at his friends. In an unsure voice, probably because it was out of character for him, Cory asked, "You two okay?"

Jonathan nodded, "Yeah, I just feel like an ass for not thinking of them as people. It's just . . . for a bit there, I was glad they were gone, but I know that's not cool of me."

"I get it, man, I get it," said Cory, sitting down in the computer chair carefully as though not knowing what else to do.

Taking a breath and squeezing his eyes shut, Jonathan did his best to center himself. Opening his eyes, he met his friend's gaze. "I'm cool now. Thanks, guys."

"Anytime. We are all friends here in good times and bad," said Trevor. A little awkwardly, Cory agreed.

"Let's just make sure we get this monster," said Jonathan as confidence began to rebuild itself.

Suddenly, he realized cold was overcoming him and goosebumps were popping up on his arm. "Is it just me, or is it getting cold in here?"

"It's not just you, man. Did your parents turn their AC into a freezer?" asked Cory, crossing his arms and rubbing them. As with a sixth sense, Jonathan felt like he was being watched. A prickle at the back of his neck sent him whipping around to look out the window.

As before, the window looked out over the town full of lights glowing brightly against the darkness of the moonless sky. The red leaves of the maple tree below his window were as dark as blood. Then Jonathan saw it: from the branches glowed two bright green eyes. They seemed to pierce Jonathan's soul. Those eyes were full of hate and murder.

He couldn't move; he felt like a person playing at being a statue as his friends talked in the background. From a long way off, their voices came to him. Cory was asking him, "You okay, man? You look like you saw a ghost."

Then, Trevor whispered, "Do you see something?"

Jonathan heard Trevor moving towards the window to get a look outside, but Jonathan was trapped in his own mind as he fought to get control of himself but nothing happened.

Jonathan screamed in his head. But the eyes stared back from the darkness, demanding Jonathan's compliance. Then just as suddenly as a light going out, the green eyes were gone, winking out of existence. Jonathan caught movement as a huge shape leapt from the tree and out of sight. There was a loud popping sound.

Jonathan's friends were staring out the window. "I thought I saw something out there, and what was that sound? Did a car backfire?" asked Cory.

As Jonathan sat down on his bed, beads of sweat were popping up all over his forehead. "You guys saw it, didn't you?"

"I thought I saw an owl or something big come out of the tree," answered Trevor. Then he continued hesitantly, "What did you see?"

"The eyes. You guys didn't see them?" he asked his perturbed friends. They both shook their heads. Jonathan looked back out the window just to prove to himself that whatever had been there was gone. Instead, Jonathan saw the man with the cane again. He was quickly walking by as he tucked something inside his vest.

"What's he doing on this side of town?" asked Trevor.

"Yeah, he doesn't look like he's from around here," added Cory.

"I don't know," Jonathan replied. "Do you guys remember the

police saying he was asking questions around the crime scene? Could he be some kind of private detective like the Pinkertons?" His friends both shrugged.

After a moment, Trevor added, "But even if he is investigating the murders, what would he be doing on the opposite side of town from where the crime took place?"

No one could come up with an accurate answer. Jonathan glanced back at his computer, wondering, *Could the monster be a werewolf, and had it just been watching me and my friends?* Then he said aloud, "I say tomorrow we go back to the scene of the crime. Now that we have a list of suspects, we know what to look for."

Trevor nodded his agreement, but Cory asked, "And what sign are we looking for?"

"Well, hair or prints of the creatures we looked up. It has not rained, so any prints would not have been washed away," answered Jonathan.

"Yeah, it couldn't hurt," said Trevor. "Let's look harder at the specific prints of these creatures."

"In other words, wolf prints would be obvious here; there would be few creatures like it. However, if it's the Annis or a ghoul, are the prints of humanoid bare feet? How are we supposed to tell them apart from just people?" asked Cory.

"Who is going to be barefoot by the river?" answered Trevor.

Jonathan was glad to have somebody that could ground his supernatural beliefs and give them a practical application. Even though they argued a lot over the occult and cryptozoological theories, Jonathan loved the interactions.

Just then, there was a sharp knock at the bedroom door before his dad opened it. "Sorry to interrupt, guys. I just wanted to get the dishes and get my son's help bringing up the air mattresses and blankets from the basement for you all."

"Of course," answered Jonathan. He sensed his dad also wanted him for something else, though. The older man's smile seemed forced, and there was a line on his brow indicating deep thought.

"We'll keep looking over these things," said Trevor, giving Jonathan a hopeful smile. Plainly he had seen Mr. Campbell's face, too, and was concerned by it.

"I'll be right back, guys. Cory, see if you can get Epona. That should make things easier."

Cory quirked a smile. "Already on my way."

Following his dad, Jonathan went down the stairs.

CHAPTER II

Jeff swatted his hand at the bat that had collided with his head. "This is so dumb," he muttered as he glanced around. His boss, Dr. Greene, was checking the mist net. Jeff was one of four interns assisting the professor as he tried to collect data from the little flying rodents. Jeff ground his teeth as a little brown bat swooped right in front of his nose.

"How is the acoustic monitoring equipment working, Starlings?" Dr. Greene asked Jeff.

"It's all good, Dr. Greene," answered Jeff in a polite voice.

Dr. Greene turned back to the other interns, helping them take blood samples and attach nano radio monitoring equipment. Jeff did his best not to give the professor his middle finger.

Pulling on the shoulder strap attached to the small bag holding the receiver, Jeff looked over the equipment, making sure it was actually working properly. The acoustic monitoring equipment gathered data on the bats using their echolocation. It gave much-needed information about which species were using Sodalis Preserve's caves.

The smell of bat guano was strong in the air, and Jeff pinched his nose. All the bats flying gave him the creeps. He shivered and ran a hand through his short blonde hair and adjusted his glasses. When he saw Dr. Greene glance at him, Jeff hurried over to attach one of his thermal cameras to a tree. *This sucks*, he thought. He could be doing such better things right now—like sleeping.

Why had he decided to write his master's thesis on the white-nose syndrome? Jeff had figured—as he had wanted to work with animals, and bats were such a big deal in this cave state—that it would be easy. And he had been right. There was plenty of research on the topic. So, taking that research and putting his own spin on it had been a breeze. If there was one thing a degree gave you, it was the ability to use Google effectively.

Now, however, he was stuck. Why would someone studying bears want somebody who had written their thesis about bats? He had effectively shot himself in the foot. It had been lucky just for him to get this internship. That was just how competitive the world of wildlife biology was. But that didn't mean he would get a paycheck. In most cases, interns did not get paid, or if they did, it wasn't enough to support yourself.

Which is the only reason he had taken the internship with Dr. Greene; it only required a few nights per month during the bat season to collect data. Jeff's actual current job was working at a restaurant back in O'Fallon. *What's the world coming to? A master's degree, and here I am, kneeling in the mud in the woods, getting information that we already know,* he mused. Everyone knew which bats were here: little brown bats, big brown bats, and the oh-so-special Indiana bat.

Jeff finished attaching the camera and checked its line of sight. Then, he stood up and looked for another location. He spotted a tree that had a good view of a cave entrance and noticed Dr. Greene showing the "special" interns how to attach the nano transmitters. Rebecca, the plump redhead from Mexico, Missouri, had shaved the bat's scapular region. Next, Dr. Greene attached the transmitter to the shaved area with eyelash adhesive.

Jeff already understood and could have done this, but of course Dr. Greene didn't ask him to do it. He instead had to do the grunt work because he was a low man on the totem pole. The other two interns actually helped Dr. Greene go over the data in "The Lab" back in Colombia, Missouri.

"Sir, doesn't the transmitter hurt the bat's air dynamics?" asked Scott Redding, the brown-haired nerd.

Of course not, four eyes, thought Jeff impatiently.

"Of course not; we would not use it if it did," answered Dr. Greene patiently.

Rolling his eyes and kicking a gumball out of his way, Jeff stomped up to another tree. He looked over his shoulder toward the others with jealousy burning.

Suddenly, he tripped and put out his hands to catch himself on the tree. In his haste, he grabbed onto something that was warm and furry. With a screech and flapping of wings, a huge bat flew into his face. Jeff fell backwards, waving his hands wildly. One hand connected with the bat, and he felt a sharp pain in his index finger. Jeff cried out and clutched his finger to his chest. It felt like the injured digit had a heartbeat as it pulsed with pain.

There were hurried footsteps, and Jeff looked up to see Dr. Greene standing over him with an angry expression on his face. "I'm sorry, sir. I tripped and cut my finger," said Jeff in a rush.

"You mean you tripped and in your clumsiness got bitten by a hoary bat—one of the first hoary bats in this area that I've heard of, and you attacked it," exclaimed Dr. Greene, his face turning red with anger.

Jeff felt himself flush with pent-up frustration. "I tripped . . . I couldn't help it!"

Dr. Greene wasn't even looking at him; he was following the hoary bat's flight with a look of concern. "Just leave the damn cameras with me. I'll finish them up. See that you don't hurt wildlife anymore," said Dr. Greene, calming as the hoary bat caught a huge lunar moth.

"What about my hand? I'm still bleeding here," said Jeff weakly.

Dr. Greene smiled as the large bat landed in another tree and began to eat the lunar moth with a ferocity that was astonishing to behold.

The professor gave Jeff a passing look before turning back to his beloved bats. "There's a medical kit under the passenger seat. Get your wound cleaned, then finish up your sound recording." Jeff held his throbbing finger to his chest as he made his way to the professor's nice Highlander. He saw the other two interns give him looks of disgust as he passed.

Jeff didn't understand it. They were all human, after all. People made mistakes. Shouldn't they be getting him to an emergency room to be treated for an animal bite? Why didn't anyone care about him? Jeff spat on the professor's window without thinking about it. Served the bat-shit crazy professor right!

"It was just a stupid hoary bat! Everyone knows they are in Missouri! What's the big freaking deal if they're here in this good-for-nothing town?" Jerking the door open, Jeff reached under the passenger seat and pulled out a white, cheap, plastic medical kit. Inside, he found some antibacterial spray and Neosporin.

Jeff sprayed his finger liberally. It stung, and he winced at the new discomfort. Using the vehicle's overhead light, he examined the bite. It really was only a scratch. Fingers always bled a lot. Then a grin came to his face. He'd get back at the professor when he sued him for allowing this to happen to him. He had a friend who had gotten into law school. "Yeah, George will fix it," he said quietly to himself.

Smiling now, Jeff put a small adhesive bandage on his finger and closed the car door with a slam. He looked up to see the other two interns walking towards him. "What's up, guys? Is everything all good?"

"Yeah, we are going to get a bite to eat. Dr. Greene said you would handle cleanup," said Rebecca tartly. She gave Jeff a look that seemed to yell, "I hate your guts."

Jeff looked between them, frowning now. He had handled the last cleanup—wasn't it someone else's turn?

"That's not a problem, is it, dude?" asked Scott cautiously.

Scott was such a little bitch. Jeff wondered if the two were having some good times. Jeff knew they weren't the ones to attack, though, and with any luck, he'd get his payback with interest on Dr. Greene. "Naw, it's cool. I got things here," said Jeff with a smile. It was so sweet to see how uncomfortable he had made the two as they passed. Just to run it in, he added, "Don't worry, I've got your backs just like you've got mine."

Walking over to the mist net, Jeff looked around. The mist net was at least unattached already from the two eight-foot poles. However, it lay sprawled out over the twenty feet between the two poles. "They couldn't at least do it in a tidy way," he said out loud. Giving a sigh, he began the arduous task of rolling up the mist net. However, he kept looking around nervously.

The clearing was quiet except for the flapping of wings and the intermittent squeaks of the multitude of bats of all sizes. The feeling of being watched was all around Jeff. He kept standing up and looking about, but his only company was the bats. Without warning, something large rushed by him. Jeff turned to lash out only to see a great-horned owl snatch a bat within feet of him.

Jeff gave the owl the finger and bent back down to his duties. Then something brushed the back of his leg. He kicked out hard and turned around swinging, expecting to find a bat, but nothing was there. Giving a roar of anger, he kicked the mist net. It became tangled around his leg, and he tripped. Falling, he hit the ground hard.

His head was spinning, and he felt something hot and wet running over his lips. Reaching up, he wiped his face. His fingers came away red in the light from his headlamp. Touching his nose, he groaned as he felt it. Then he froze. Had he just heard someone calling for him?

"Oh shit, I forgot the professor is still here," he said, kicking himself. Jeff had been so pissed about doing cleanup again he had completely forgotten about the old man. "Where the hell did he get to?" he muttered.

Then he said in a near shout, "Dr. Greene, where are you? Do you need help?"

Jeff really didn't care about the old man. But he thought if he helped him while the other two were off getting "food," he would then be number one. Also, if he was in better standing with the professor, it could lead to better things—maybe even a conservation job that was not only exciting but also paid well!

Exhilarated, he quickly got his feet untangled while listening with all his might. Off to his right, he heard what sounded like a groan. "Professor, I'm coming," he explained, hurrying over. His light didn't show him anything, but Jeff knew it had to be the professor. His injuries forgotten, Jeff smiled as he pushed past a low-hanging branch.

"I'm over here," said Dr. Greene in a weak voice.

The voice had come from deeper in the woods. Jeff couldn't see the professor yet in his headlamp's illumination, but that didn't matter. "I'm coming, Dr. Greene. Just keep making noise so I can find you." Jeff pushed past bushes, and at one point, a tree caught his backpack with the antenna for the acoustic equipment.

Putting the pack down, he again heard Dr. Greene's voice, closer now but off to his left: "You're a lifesaver, kid." Grinning in spite of the scrapes from the bushes and trees, Jeff pushed on.

Suddenly, his headlamp was torn from his head by a tree branch that felt like skeletal fingers. The light went out, and Jeff panicked, trying to find the light. He shouted out, "Dr. Greene, I lost my light. Where are you?"

"Right here," said Dr. Greene, his hand falling onto Jeff's shoulder. Jeff sighed with relief and reached up to take the professor's hand off his shoulder because it was just weird. He did not roll that way.

But Dr. Greene's hand felt wrong. Jeff felt something sticky on his fingers. He took his hand away and wiped his fingers on his pants. "Professor, what the heck did you get into?" Then Dr. Greene's hand fell from Jeff's shoulder. He heard the appendage hit the ground with a gross, wet *thwack*. Jeff screamed and made to run, but a strong tree branch had hooked into his shirt.

Jeff turned to pull himself free. Grabbing the branch, he found his hand closing over impossibly long fingers. Screaming again, Jeff fought wildly, kicking out at whoever had him. Instead, his leg was grabbed, as well, by nails that felt like talons biting into him. Jeff felt himself being lifted by his bleeding leg. He cried out and struggled, but he couldn't break free. Then he felt a hot, putrid breath inches from his face.

"Thank you for the meal," said Dr. Greene's voice.

CHAPTER 12

In the living room, Jonathan's mom had the news on. Her dark hair was thrown over one shoulder as she read from her Kindle. She smiled at her son and husband as they took care of the dishes. "Everybody having a good time?" she asked.

"Of course! Pizza and games are always good," Jonathan answered with a genuine smile. Having finished the dishes and wiping up, he followed his dad as they made their way to the basement. Mr. Campbell kissed his wife, and Jonathan saw a look of concern pass between them.

Jonathan gave his mom a kiss on the cheek and whispered, "Is everything okay? Is somebody trying to buy the shop out again?"

She smiled at him and looked down at her Kindle. Jonathan thought he saw tears in her eyes. However, her voice was normal as she answered, "I'm fine. Your father just needs to talk to you."

Jonathan, more perturbed than ever, followed his dad down the steps. For some reason, Jonathan felt nervous, but he couldn't remember doing something bad to earn a tongue lashing. The wooden stairs creaked as Jonathan walked down into the unfinished basement, which was cold as ever and dark. It made Jonathan feel like he was descending into a cave. From the other side of the basement, he could hear the rumble of the washer and dryer.

Jonathan listened as his dad crossed to the light switch and flicked on the overhead bulbs. Jonathan took in a breath of astonishment. Their pool table sat in the middle of the room, the balls set up for a game. However, in the middle of the table lay the ancient, antler-handled knife next to its sheath. Jonathan's eyes shot to his father's as fast as an arrow. His eyes weren't angry or stern; they were soft and full of concern.

"Dad, what's—" started Jonathan, but his father put up a hand to silence him.

Then his father asked, "How much do you know of our family history?"

"That we're mutts, just like most Americans," Jonathan quipped, trying to break the tension.

"I'm serious. Jonathan Campbell, what do you already know?" his father's voice was calm, but there was a strength behind it that allowed no argument. It was really out of character for his dad to be so serious.

Taking a breath, Jonathan began, "On Mom's side, her father's family was mostly English and German. While on her mother's side, we know her great-grandmother was full Cherokee. Her great-grandmother came west on the Trail of Tears until she died in Southern Missouri. Her husband was not full Cherokee, so he kept the children with him instead of going to a reservation. After that, her family mixed with the people around them."

His father nodded sharply and asked, "And what about on my side?"

Jonathan hesitated, then he went on, gesturing at the knife, "I know that Grandpa always said he was from the Ojibwe tribe. I think they lived somewhere around the Michigan and Canada border. Grandma's family were German; they did a lot of farming around Pennsylvania."

"Yes, I was asking for the CliffsNotes version, and you nailed it." His stern face gave a small smile.

"I don't know why Grandpa didn't stay with the tribe or anything about that, though. I don't even know in detail what the Ojibwe or

Cherokee believed, apart from believing that all nature is made up of good and bad spirits," Jonathan responded, frustrated. His dad seemed to deflate.

"According to Algonquin beliefs, the world around us, such as the plants and stones, are inhabited by the spirits that influence others. We call these powerful spirits the Manitous, and we do our best to appease them. Many of these Manitous can be evil, so we fight to resist those. You will often hear of people talking about 'The Great Spirit'—we call it the Kitcki Manitou."

"Okay, but we don't do any of that, right?" asked Jonathan.

"Good question," said his father with a subtle smile. "The Ojibwe and some others found it easier than other Native American groups to adopt Christianity because they already believed in one God."

Jonathan nodded, then asked, "But what does any of that have to do with Grandpa or the knife?" Jonathan stole a glance at the knife, curious.

"What do you know of the Sandy Lake tragedy of eighteen fifty?" asked his father sadly. Jonathan's confused look was answer enough.

"So basically, treaty payments were promised if the Ojibwe moved to Sandy Lake. However, when they arrived, there were little to no supplies, and no one was even there to give out the supplies that were there. Then, the winter hit, and hundreds of the Ojibwe lost their lives."

"Why have I never heard of this, and again, where is this all going?" asked Jonathan. He felt some part of him going angry at the long-past injustice.

His father put up a placating hand as though asking for patience. "With the Trail of Tears going on around the same time, other tragedies have gotten passed over." Jonathan nodded his understanding, but still, people had lost their lives. Any life should not be forgotten so easily. "Our family were among the Ojibwe that were present. Your great-grandfather was a shaman. With the subsequent starvation at Sandy Lake, the spirits of the cannibal Manitous became active."

Jonathan frowned. Was his father talking about what he thought he was?

His father gave him a knowing look. "You know what that means, don't you?" he asked. Jonathan nodded slowly. "Many wendigo were made in the following winters. It fell on people like your great-grandfather to hunt down and destroy them."

Taking up the knife, he showed it to Jonathan. "This knife has been passed down, father to son, to combat the dark creatures of this world." Mr. Campbell's face was so stiff it looked like it was made of stone. He held out the knife to Jonathan, hilt first. With shaking fingers, Jonathan took the weapon. "With everything going on in the world, we must be strong, Jonathan. Stand up for those who cannot stand against the darkness."

"I don't understand," said Jonathan as he gazed at the razor edge of the dark blade. He gripped the knife's handle and felt his fingers find the places where other fingers had gripped it. Jonathan felt a warm feeling coming over him. A sense of purpose was cementing itself inside him. He would stand as his family had stood before him against whatever this "darkness" was.

Adam's hand fell on Jonathan's shoulder, comforting him. Jonathan looked up into his father's dark-brown eyes. He smiled at his son and handed him the knife's sheath. Carved into the old leather were symbols of the many animals of the wood. The leather was warm and smooth in Jonathan's hand.

"Your grandfather made this. I know you will make our family proud," his father said.

"But how will I know what I have to do? Or how to do it? I don't know anything about using a knife to fight someone . . . or some*thing*."

"You'll just have to trust me," his father replied. "Somehow in our family, we just seem to *know*."

"You think it's a wendigo that killed the kids from my school, don't you?"

"I . . ." Adam began, "I can't really tell you more about it right now. There's something I have to do first. But you will know more soon."

Jonathan could see the set to his father's jaw and knew it would be pointless to ask for any more details right then. He told himself to be patient, but it was hard to do so.

"Now then, what do you say we get those air mattresses?" his father said, abruptly changing the subject.

"Of course—we wouldn't want to sleep on the floor," laughed Jonathan. His father chuckled as well, breaking the tension.

Leading the way, his father opened the wood door in the corner of the basement that led to a space used as a storage area and laundry room. Jonathan, a little stunned with the sudden honor his father had bestowed upon him, undid his belt and hooked the knife so it hung on his right side. Something felt right about that, as though it was meant to be on his hip. Looking up, Jonathan could see his family's garage, which was not attached to the house, through the above-ground windows. Inside, in the back, Jonathan knew there was a large locker containing guns. He hoped he wouldn't need those, though. With his friends at his side, they would find out who had killed Amanda and Chris and put a stop to them . . . or it.

He felt full of purpose now. He could actually feel his courage mounting as though it were a physical thing. He could be the one to stand against the darkness just as his family had. Feeling bold and brave, knowing he could succeed, he said aloud, "I *will* do it!"

Then there came a grunt from his father. Jonathan was jolted out of his inner thoughts and hurried forward to help him.

CHAPTER 13

Minutes later, the two arrived back in Jonathan's room.

"Well, don't just stand there—help me unroll these," said Jonathan, breathing a little harder after climbing the stairs while carrying two of the rolled-up air mattresses.

His friends had been looking out the window, talking quietly. Mr. Campbell smiled and set down his own air mattress and began to unwind the air pump's cord.

"Of course," said Trevor, hurrying over to take one of the mattresses. Cory curled an eyebrow at Jonathan and noted, "If your lanky butt is that tired from a few stairs, then you need more exercise."

"You guys play nice, or I'll send Mrs. Campbell up to settle things."

They all chuckled, and Mr. Campbell left the room, wishing them all a good night. Jonathan quietly hurried to the door to listen as his father creaked down the stairs.

Cory began, "What are you—" but Jonathan broke off his question with a hand gesturing for silence.

As his father descended the last few stairs, Jonathan heard the ring of a cell phone. His father's voice answered, "Yeah, Cecil, did you get it?" There was a long pause, then, "What the hell do you mean you missed? You said you had it under control, Cecil!" Then his father's voice became fainter, and Jonathan couldn't make out much else of what his parents' muffled voices were saying.

Jonathan turned back to his friends as Cory said, "What the heck was all that about, and why'd you hush me?"

Before Jonathan could answer, Trevor added, "And why do you have that knife?"

Jonathan smiled. "My dad gave it to me. He said it was used by my ancestors to—in his words—drive back the darkness."

Trevor mouthed a "Wow!" in return as Jonathan showed them the drawn knife.

"That's cool and all, but what does he mean by 'the darkness'?" said Cory, putting a scary pitch to the last part.

"Yeah, and what ancestors? Your Native American ones?'" asked Trevor.

"Yes, those ancestors, but I honestly don't know myself what it all means," answered Jonathan. "My dad wouldn't tell me everything yet. What he would tell me, however, was about the wendigo."

So Jonathan explained what his father had said about the ancient foe and his family's role in killing the wendigo.

Several minutes later, Jonathan, now wanting to get off the subject, gestured to the windows. "What were you two discussing when I came back?" His friends looked at each other, and Cory gave a slight nod with a face that seemed resigned.

"We were talking about sneaking out tonight," said Trevor in a nervous tone.

Jonathan grinned, "That's just what I was thinking. But how are we going to do it?"

"I don't think that's going to be a problem," stated Cory as he looked out the window. Jonathan followed his gaze to see his parents' van driving away. He wondered what they could be up to and who this Cecil person was.

Then he shrugged. "Well, at least that's one problem we don't have to worry about."

Turning, the three went out of Jonathan's room and rumbled down the stairs, not taking another moment to think about what they were doing. It was so exciting, even though Jonathan realized it was dumb and possibly dangerous. But it was his moment.

Everyone talks of moments they had let pass by. *And I'm not letting this go! It's my time*, thought Jonathan as he burst through the front door. His parents were gone; the van was nowhere in sight. He looked down the road the way his parents had gone, wondering, *Could the reason we are sneaking out and why my parents drove off be related?*

"Shouldn't we have something besides one knife to defend ourselves?" said Cory, his voice quiet but high-pitched, breaking in on Jonathan's thoughts.

"Right," said Jonathan, now realizing that other weapons actually would be helpful. He led his friends to the garage and put in the pass code. The door lifted agonizingly slowly.

Once it was open just enough, he impatiently ducked under the door as it continued to rise. To do this, his lanky frame bent in half, and his hands brushed the cold cement floor. He hurried over to a bunch of sports equipment that was stacked haphazardly in one corner like something long dejected, which was not too far from the truth. Picking up a metal baseball bat, Jonathan swung it and flipped it around as though it were some kind of sword he was using. Turning to his friends, he grinned. "Batter up!" With a flip, Jonathan handed the bat, handle first, to Trevor, who grinned in return.

Cory cleared his throat, and the other two looked around at him. Jonathan quirked an eyebrow in question. "I'm just saying we could have had something better than bats," said Cory, gesturing at the gun safe, its door shockingly ajar.

As Jonathan stepped up to the safe, alarm bells were going off in his head. "What the hell is going on?" he wanted to scream.

There was empty space where five guns should have been: two Mossberg twelve-gauge shotguns, one Knight's SR-25 rifle that was seven-point-six-two caliber with a twenty-inch suppressor and a thermal scope, and two forty-caliber Smith and Wessons. Jonathan's parents had taught him about gun safety since he was small, and they had often gone to the shooting range as a family. So Jonathan knew all about the guns and ammo that should have been in the safe.

"Looks like your parents went hunting, too," said Trevor.

That was an understatement. It looked more like his parents were going to war or something. Jonathan wanted to scream, or run, or fight, or even cry. But he couldn't do any of those, so he just stood there, dumbstruck. If they were going to track this thing down, and his dad had given him the knife, why hadn't they told him? Wasn't he part of this now? Then, he felt the knife at his waist, and his earlier certainty stole over him again. His parents were out there, and he was standing here, useless. It was time to get moving.

"Whatever is going on, let's get to the bottom of it," he said as determination swelled.

"Right. Let's do it," nodded Trevor, also determined. He and Jonathan looked at Cory, who was looking at the remaining items in the gun locker. There were a bunch of ammo boxes that had been knocked askew, presumably in Jonathan's parents' rush. Then he smiled, spotting something he had apparently been looking for.

Bending down, he picked something up, a large can of some kind. Showing it to the others, he smiled again. "One spray of this will stop anything in its tracks!" It was a can of bear spray. "Your parents won't mind if I borrow this, will they?" he asked.

"Of course not. Let's do this shit! Ain't nobody stopping us!"

The three teens laughed, all traces of nervousness gone in the adrenaline rush of actually doing something so audacious.

Jonathan just knew that he had to do this. He had to help his parents . . . before there were more deaths. So, the boys stole out of the garage, shutting its door behind them as they left. Jonathan looked at his old-school flip phone to check the time and for any messages. It said *9:03 p.m.*, and he saw one message from his mom: *Love you, hun. Had to go out for a bit. Help yourselves to any of the snack stuff and sodas. Don't wait up. We'll be out late.*

Just in case this was all some misunderstanding, which he doubted, he fired off his reply: *Thanks. I'll leave the hall light on for you. Love you, too.*

CHAPTER 14

Adam Campbell pulled the van up next to the curb where his old friend Cecil stood waiting. Glancing at his constant partner and love of his life, he gave Barbara a reassuring grin. She grinned back, but her game face was on, and it was forced. Opening the door and stepping out of the van, she started in on Cecil right away, "We told you and the company we were done. How could you let these things happen?"

Cecil, usually unflappable, frowned deeply, the well-bred English features of his face looking tired. He wasn't a tall man or short. Besides the fact that he wore clothes more suited to a college professor, he was unremarkable, except for his hazel eyes, which just now blazed with passion and anxious energy. "I came as soon as I heard, Barbara. I'm sorry to have involved you two again, but I need you on this."

Adam got out of the vehicle, as well, and headed to the rear of the van. Putting on a heavy vest bursting with shotgun shells on one side and his Smith and Wesson cartridges on the other, he wordlessly grabbed his shotgun and began to load it. As he put down the shotgun and reached for his pistol, a strong hand clasped his shoulder. Looking up, he met Cecil's now-earnest gaze.

"Seriously, both of you, I never would have let this happen if I had known. But you were our best tracker, Adam, and we must get this contained before this monster kills again. We have to contain this mess."

Letting out a breath, Adam answered tiredly, "I know, my old friend. Let's get this fixed." Barbara made to say something, but Adam cut her off. "Too many have died already. This is our home, and no monster from hell itself will threaten our boy!"

Barbara nodded, her eyes welling with tears, but she fought them back and reached into the trunk and pulled out her ammo belt for her rifle, securing it around her waist. Grabbing a magazine next, she put it in place with a loud *clack*.

The three each gave one decisive nod to their companions. Anything that needed to be said could be said later. Right now, there was a job to do. Checking that his handgun was loaded, Adam put it in a holster on his belt on his left side. Finally, he picked up his trusty tomahawk and put in its rightful place on his belt on his right side.

He looked up to see Cecil pulling out his own weapon, an ancient Webley Mk IV. Though it was old, Cecil had said a soldier had used it in World War Two.

"When are you going to give up on that fossil?" Adam quipped.

Cecil looked up and grinned at him. "When it lets me down. And . . . I have upgraded," he said, flicking a hidden switch on his cane. The wooden shaft opened up, and a trigger dropped down.

Cecil then tugged on the gold ornament at the grip, and it came off with a pop. He pulled out a buttstock and snapped it into place. Then, he snapped it up into a hidden slot in the wood. The handle was a magazine!

"Damn, what's it take?" asked Adam, honestly curious.

"Seven point six two, and it's semi-automatic. Had a clever gunsmith make it for me," Cecil answered proudly.

Removing the front of the gun with a twist and a mechanized snap revealed the end of the gun from what had been the tip of the cane. Finally, with a snort of approval Cecil snapped the piece into place for a forearm grip.

"What do you do when your hidden magazine runs out?" asked Barbara.

Pulling open his tweed vest, he showed off several hidden magazines on the inside of the garment. "The vest is coarse lined with Kevlar," added Cecil with a wink.

Then, he led the way through the gate in the fence of the old beat-up house. Adam noted the spots of blood here and there leading to the gate. He also took in the monster's stride. It was impressive. At the top of the fence, there was a large splash of blood that stained the old wood, and at the top, some of the wood had been splintered off in the monster's apparent rush.

"I followed the bastard as best I could, but I know when I'm out of my depth," Cecil said. Adam nodded his understanding and pumped a shotgun round into place. He heard Barbara behind him. Her breathing was slow, and he knew she had his back, her own pistol at the ready.

Cecil moved to the gate and eased the latch up. His back to the fence, he gave Adam a nod. Without a second thought, he kicked the gate open and burst through. His eyes flicked left, right, up, and down. More blood colored the grass, and two blood-stained metal garbage cans, their refuse spilling out, lay dented on their sides. The creature must have fallen. Then Cecil sucked in a breath of shock. The body of a balding, overweight man lay a few feet ahead.

The man's throat was torn away, and his intestines were spilling out of him from the monster's vicious attack. Without looking too hard, Adam knew several organs were missing. He heard Barbara taking shallow breaths, and Cecil moved up next to Adam, his gun at the ready.

"Barbara, keep the woods covered and don't separate from us," whispered Cecil. Then, in a rush, he jumped cat-like around the side of the house and looked around.

"Clear," he whispered and hurried away.

Adam hurried after him. The trail of blood led to the wall of the house. Bloody, elongated hand- and footprints showed where their quarry had climbed up the wall. Following the prints, Adam found they made their way to just above the back sliding glass door, which had been broken inwards. He very briefly closed his eyes and took a deep breath to steady his nerves. He knew what he was going to see.

Opening his eyes, he saw Cecil check the woman's pulse. She lay in a pool of blood on top of the broken glass from the door. Cecil took off his fedora with a growl and set it down on the countertop as he entered the house past the woman. He did this as though acknowledging that this nicety still needed to be observed.

"Is she . . .?" whispered Barbara hesitantly, her eyes on the woods.

"Gone," Adam answered sadly.

Cecil was looking around the kitchen, his blue eyes trying to take everything in.

Besides the body of the woman, which Adam found hard to look at, the room was scrupulously clean. A pair of yellow gloves and a wash cloth sat abandoned on the edge of the sink. Here and there were memories of this family. Memories that meant something to the two people. Now, what were the items but something that would probably go to fill some landfill or find themselves gathering dust in an antique store? Then, Cecil rushed past Adam, his gun low and cane clacking on the old wood floor. He hurried to look out the door and cursed.

"I've got nothing out here," said Barbara. "On your toes, both of you. I can't find any trace of it."

Adam, despite his distaste of the sight of the woman, stepped over to her and bent down at her side and took a good look at her. Like her husband, she was middle-aged and slightly overweight. She wore a white nightdress, stained red by what must have been four claws ripping her open from right collarbone to left hip. Her breasts lay limp and sagging. The woman's hair was graying, and her head was turned at an odd angle.

Adam paused, and he heard the other two behind him looking

around, protecting his back as he went through what had happened here in his mind. The creature was big, and it had been injured. Cecil, knowing the wendigo would be drawn to the Campbells' home, had staked it out. When the creature appeared there, he had shot it in the right shoulder with his powerful, large-caliber rifle that he had left behind for Adam to pick up. Cecil had then followed the wounded monster to this house and called Adam for backup.

From the broken fence, it was apparent that the creature had been in a hurry. It had lost its balance and crashed into the garbage cans. The man had obviously rushed out to investigate and had been killed.

Then, the creature must have heard the woman call for her husband. Most likely, it had climbed the wall to sneak up on the woman when she came outside. Adam now looked hard at the woman. There was less blood than he had originally thought around her body. Looking back outside, he saw the puddle of blood there was much more substantial. He had first thought she had been thrown through the door and then torn open.

However, that wasn't what the blood said. Her neck had been broken first. The creature must have dropped down behind the woman as she exited through the doorway, and then it broke her neck. After that, it slashed the woman, took what it wanted from her, and threw her body through the door into the house. But why throw her?

Looking more closely around the room, Adam stood up. Nothing was out of order. Then a thought struck him, and he glanced around at Cecil so fast his neck popped. He was outside, staring down with horror at a patch of grass near the edge of the trees. Even from where Adam stood, he could tell the grass was stained red with blood. Their eyes met, and both understood they had been tricked.

The monster had healed itself. Of course it had. All its kind healed like Wolverine. It had deliberately led them here and set up this grizzly murder scene just for them. *I guess this is why I should have stayed in retirement. I'm too rusty*, thought Adam bitterly. Even as he had this thought, he heard a soft sound from right behind him.

That was all the warning he got. Adam spun his gun up and ready, but he was too slow. A huge, pale figure blurred towards Adam and swung one long-fingered, clawed hand at him. Swinging the butt of his weapon up to block the slash, Adam at the same time cried out a warning. He was just fast enough to hit the monster's wrist, slowing its blow so at least it didn't kill him. The blow meant to disembowel Adam hit his arm instead, just above the elbow.

Adam was flung to the ground, and he felt his shoulder pop out of place. He screamed and rolled. Even as he rolled, he heard the *bark-bark* of Cecil's revolver. The creature screamed so loud that Adam heard glass shatter and his ear drums throbbed painfully. His right arm numb from the blow, he pulled out his tomahawk with his left. Pushing off with his legs, Adam spun and swung upwards at the ghastly white form above him. His blade caught the creature in the back of its knee.

The creature, with all its power, pulled its leg forward, tearing the tomahawk from both its leg and Adam's hand. The tomahawk went spinning across the blood-splattered floor. Adam again pushed off with his legs, away from the creature, drawing his hand gun with a scream of pain from his injured arm.

Cecil shot his remaining rounds into the creature's emaciated chest. There was a snap as Cecil flipped down the front of his gun to reload. He cursed loudly, adding, "You know how to take the lead; I'll give you that, mate!"

As Adam raised his gun, his reflexes felt sluggish, and a chill ran through him. His breath suddenly came out as fog, and goosebumps popped up on his arms and legs. The creature, apparently unconcerned, turned to Adam. Cecil's bullets had punched holes through its chest. However, in the space of a heartbeat, the holes closed over with new flesh. The creature gave Adam a bloody grin of sharp and broken teeth.

Adam had a sudden flash of inspiration and snapped his weapon down and shot the monster through its still-wounded knee. He could have kicked himself. He well knew the history of this creature, and yet he had forgotten about his own special weapons. The creature fell over its crumpled knee, and Adam leapt to his feet, moving quick as a heartbeat towards his fallen tomahawk to finish it. However, still as fast as ever, the creature met his leap with a fist to Adam's stomach that threw him, cracking the kitchen wall behind.

All the air was gone from Adam's lungs, and he labored to catch his breath. He had no strength in him and couldn't even roll over to protect himself. Giving himself up for dead as he heard the creature scrabbling after him, Adam closed his stinging eyes. Then, there was a loud thump and a louder crash followed by an ear-splitting scream. Relaxing his muscles at last with an effort, Adam rolled over.

The creature was gone! Where it had been was a hole in the wall. Barbara stood just outside, her rifle raised to shoot again. Adam grinned though his body screamed in pain from his injuries. Glancing back through the hole, Adam saw that the creature stood on its good leg, its hands acting like crutches. It looked to Adam like a deformed chimp that had just gotten its ass kicked.

It hissed at them, and then to the man's surprise spoke in a choking voice: "I am death and hunger. Your blood will satisfy me for only moments."

A quickly healing hole could be seen high on its right shoulder. *God, the healing factor is fast*, thought Adam. Then, it burst through the front door with a loud bang that made Adam's ears ring and head hurt. An echoing scream came back to Adam, and he looked around to see Cecil, his gun raised and a small smile on his face. In answer to Adam's look, Cecil said, "Tracking bullet." He grinned wider and put out a hand to Adam. "On your feet, Sitting Bull. We've got a big one."

Adam grinned back. "I'm not Sitting Bull, and you ain't no Custer." They both laughed, and Adam got to his feet, wincing in pain.

CHAPTER 15

Jonathan and his friends walked down Main Street, doing their best to look like they belonged out and about. He could see other teens gathered around the ice cream store. A few others sat in cars, making out, including a plump redhead chick and a nerdy teen with a five-o'clock shadow. They were sitting in a beat-up old car with what seemed like a metric ton of stickers on it. Along with the classic "Coexist" sticker, the others were mostly bat themed, like one depicting bats giving a hug and saying "I am darkness," and another with the words *bat Xing*. There was even one that had the Bacardi logo, with its stylized fruit bat.

Jonathan cocked his head at the car and said, "You think more bat scientists or just bat huggers?"

"I don't know. They could be some biologists," answered Trevor.

Then Cory blurted, "What the hell do you mean 'bat huggers'?!"

Jonathan flushed with embarrassment and stuttered, "You know—like tree huggers but for bats."

Cory rolled his eyes, and Jonathan playfully shoved him with a shoulder.

The boys broke into laughter, which was cut off suddenly when they saw bullies from school gathered around a yellow Camaro IROC-Z with the T-tops off. Jonathan and his friends did their best to hurry past unnoticed. Hopefully, those guys were so busy listening to Korn that they wouldn't see them. When Jonathan didn't hear any shouts or see any empty soda cans thrown at them, he thought they must be home free.

"At least they didn't catch us," said Cory, nervously looking over his shoulder.

"It's funny—we will hunt a monster, but when it comes to bullies, we sneak around and avoid them," said Trevor with a grin.

"Well, you're not me," answered Cory.

"You're right; we are not midgets," laughed Jonathan.

His friends laughed as well, and Cory stuck his tongue out at the other two. They were nearing the end of the road, and Jonathan began to feel an air of confidence stealing over him.

They passed by a Jeep full of teens with speakers blaring "Hero" by Skillet. With guitar and drums prominent in the mix, Jonathan found his head bobbing along to the music. "I can be a hero. I can do this," he thought, and a smile came to his lips.

Trevor looked at Jonathan. "Yeah, you can't deny Christian rock certainly makes you feel something."

Jonathan nodded his agreement, then his phone pinged. A notification of a text from his mom appeared: *Are you boys doing okay?* Jonathan replied that they were doing fine. However, he wondered if she had come home to find them not there and was actually fishing for information. "Well, whatever. Let's get this done," he said out loud.

"Da da-dun dunt, three nerdy teens to the rescue," blurted Cory. With a few chuckles and a couple of eye rolls, they went into the woods to follow Bear Creek for a second time that day.

Walking along the paved trail with the creek bubbling away nearby was so peaceful. Jonathan found it hard to keep up the fire he had made of his confidence. The three teens got more and more quiet as they walked, except for when an owl hooted nearby.

"Isn't that a Great Horned Owl?" asked Trevor.

"Of course not; it's a Barred Owl," answered Jonathan. Then he put on a know-it-all, simpering voice and went on, "Always remember 'Who cooks for you? Who cooks for us all?'"

With a few sputters escaping, they tried their best to stifle their laughter. Finally mastering himself, Jonathan reproached in a whisper, "We've got to be quiet, or all we will catch out here are these damn mosquitoes." As he spoke, he smacked one of the tiny vampires on Trevor's arm.

"Ow! Not so hard, man," he complained. Jonathan put up his hands in apology.

"Look, guys!" said Cory excitedly. He pointed to a group of insects hovering over the creek like fairy lights.

"So what? They're fireflies. We used to catch them all the time. What's so special about them?" asked Trevor as they walked on.

Jonathan answered him because Cory was looking back at the fireflies with the look of a person remembering something that made them happy. "Light pollution, pesticides, and of course habitat loss have driven the fireflies to near disappearing."

Trevor frowned deeply, his voice sad and pleading, "But they're fireflies. Think of all the children who will never know what it was like to see them, to be spellbound by how pretty they are."

"Most people are so busy with their own lives that it's hard for them to care," answered Cory.

Jonathan nodded. "Exactly. By the time people notice something is wrong, the species is already on a decline."

Trevor sighed, "It just sucks."

Jonathan looked towards the water. Dark shapes moved beneath it, probably crawdads and small fish, but there was the sound of something bigger moving through the water, too.

The three friends stopped dead, all looking downstream. There, on the other side of the creek, a robust raccoon was cleaning his front paws.

"Must have caught some nice crawdads," said Jonathan, smiling.

"Yeah, he's a big sucker, ain't he?" laughed Cory loudly. The two others shushed him, but the damage was done. The overly large trash panda stared at them with beady eyes. Then, apparently unafraid, waddled off into the undergrowth. They all guffawed at that before trying to stifle each other again, big dorky smiles shining on their faces.

Walking on, Jonathan was struck after a moment by how cold it felt. A breeze here, next to the creek, was common. However, it was still summer, and it shouldn't feel like the middle of autumn. Thinking back, he remembered feeling cold earlier that day, as well.

"Do you guys feel that?" he asked quietly.

The others looked at him quizzically. "There is always a breeze here. Don't be a pansy," said Cory scornfully.

Trevor gave Cory a disapproving look but added, "Yeah, man, it's just the weather. Maybe we just hit a cold spot," as he glanced up at the sky. He frowned at the absence of clouds there but shrugged it away.

Jonathan, feeling really nervous, now took a deep breath through his nose. There was a strange odor in the air. He didn't know why, but it gave him an unpleasant feeling. Then he got it. He had smelled this before, when his father had taken him hunting and had taught Jonathan to process a kill. "It's blood! I smell blood!"

The other two whipped their heads around, but Jonathan was already moving. "Johnny-boy, where are you going?" asked Cory, puzzled.

"Just follow me," Jonathan said, not even checking to see if they were doing so as he pushed his way past low-hanging branches.

Shoving his way through the woods, Jonathan could hear his friends muttering behind him. "I swear I know where I'm going," he said aloud. *And hopefully that's true*, he thought to himself. He heard Cory say something about stupid dogs when they catch a scent.

"Just shut up, man. He knows what he's doing," Trevor shot back. Then, much quieter, as though to himself, "At least I hope so."

They continued to make their way along by grasping limbs and small bushes. The flora seemed to be doing its best to slow them down or turn them aside. However, Jonathan could feel it, whatever "it" was. And the smell, the somewhat metallic tinge to the air, was getting stronger. Then a scream of pain and anguish shattered the night. Without stopping to consider his actions, Jonathan took off as fast as he could with Trevor hard on his heels.

CHAPTER 16

The branches whipped past Jonathan, some giving him stinging slaps as he hurtled through the woods with Trevor by his side. Trevor's eyes were wide with excitement and adrenaline. He could hear Cory cursing as he attempted, with his short legs, to keep up. Jonathan and Trevor were both tall and much more actively inclined.

Fighting back fear, Jonathan attempted to push a large limb to the side. But Trevor burst through the limbs and small clinging branches without a care for himself. In fact, Jonathan saw streaks of blood running down Trevor's face like red tears. Then he heard why Trevor was in such a hurry.

"Come on, guys, this isn't funny. I'll—" but the shrill voice was cut off mid-word. It was Neal. Someone was beating up poor Neal again, and like always, the white knight, Trevor, was off to save him, to Trevor's own detriment.

Neal had probably come out to see the bats. Plus, there was always a chance that if you came at the right time, you might catch some biologists at work. Since he was such a geek about the world of biology and those who studied the flora and fauna (but especially the bats), Neal may have heard of a bat-netting event on one of the Missouri Conservation sites.

Jonathan was brought out of his thoughts by a bush of some

kind whipping across his shin. The pain was white hot for a moment, and he winced. However, he didn't shout and give himself away. This was Trevor's moment. As he came to the edge of the main area of the amphitheater, Jonathan paused and watched as Trevor sprinted to the rescue, his baseball bat raised.

"What are you doing? We've got to help him," wheezed Cory. He shoved Jonathan's shoulder hard and ran to help Trevor.

Jonathan shook himself, asking out loud, "What the hell am I doing? I can't let him face those guys on his own. What type of friend am I?" Running after Trevor and Cory, he continued to chide himself. Also, something in the back of his mind sensed he was being watched.

It had gotten still colder, and the scent of blood was stronger than ever, but now it was accompanied by something that smelled like death, like bloated bodies and putrefaction. Alongside these odors was the ever-present smell of bat guano. However, the thing that hit hardest was a feeling of wrongness. Something wasn't right here. His instincts screamed at him to stop what he was doing and defend himself from whatever was making him feel this way. But his friends needed him, and Jonathan could not turn his back on them.

Suddenly, a large brown bat flew inches from his face. Jonathan flinched back and tripped. In a panic, he sprang to his feet in time to see Trevor reach the bullies. Trevor ran up to them, his bat poised like a golf club to be swung, and hit Jake hard on the back of his knee. Jake fell to the ground with a cry of pain, and Jonathan put his head down to sprint as fast as he could. As he approached the now-yelling teens, he raised his own bat and yelled in challenge. Brandon took a swing at him, but with Jonathan's long arms, he managed to crack Brandon in the ribs with his bat.

Then someone hit him in his kidneys, and Jonathan went down hard on his face. Doubled over in pain and trying to catch his breath, he rolled over onto his back. When he opened his eyes again, he saw his two friends were down and Neal was running off—hopefully, to call for help. Jonathan next saw three bullies standing over him, peering down. Jake, holding one of his legs up as though it pained him, leaned on Josh, who was helping to hold him up. Jonathan hoped it was broken. He gulped and tried to stand, but Josh kicked him in his ribs.

Jonathan tried to thrust the bat's tip into Jake's gut, but Jake dodged it, stumbling back, and cried out as he put pressure on his injured leg, "You damn asshole!"

"You couldn't leave well enough alone, could you?" said Josh, turning suddenly and kicking Trevor twice in the stomach. Trevor heaved and vomited in pain. All three bullies laughed. Jonathan tried to leap to Trevor's aid, but Brandon grabbed Jonathan's bat with one hand and with the other punched him in the nose.

Jonathan could feel his nose swelling up and hot blood in his mouth. His eyes were stinging, and though he didn't want to, he felt tears running down his cheeks. Then he felt someone pulling at his belt.

"What have we here?" gloated one of the bullies, probably Brandon the jerk. In spite of the pain and tears, Jonathan forced his eyes open. Brandon was holding his knife, and the other two laughed.

"The nerd got a knife. Woooo, so scary," chortled Josh.

"Give it back," croaked Jonathan. But the others only laughed harder. Brandon, still laughing, put his index finger to the point of the blade, barely touching it. Even so, Jonathan saw blood well up.

"Crap! Stupid knife," cursed Brandon, throwing the knife down in the dirt somewhere behind Jonathan. Staring past the bullies, Jonathan felt his heart stop.

Hundreds of bats swooped and flapped overhead, their silhouettes dark against the white moon. However, that wasn't what had scared Jonathan. In a tree, perfectly visible was a face straight out of his nightmare and Native American folklore. Its face was as white as the moon with envious green eyes shining out from it. The skin was tight, like something emaciated. It smiled with bloody, inhumanly sharp teeth.

It was a wendigo!

To Jonathan's horror, the wendigo leapt into the amphitheater to land just behind the three bullies. The creature was huge, nine feet tall, Jonathan guessed, and painfully gaunt. Its head sat on a thin, elongated neck. The arms and legs were also elongated and bone thin, and its overly large hands ended in two-inch-long, claw-like nails. Jonathan's eyes trailed down the wendigo's naked body with horror. His eyes stopped on the monster's concave stomach; he didn't want to look any lower. Just like the rest of it, the wendigo's body was skeletal, with every bone visible, especially its ribs and pelvis.

Jack started to turn his head to see what was behind him, but it was too late. The wendigo's head shot forward like a snapping turtle's and tore out what must have been Jack's jugular. Blood sprayed Jonathan like a fountain, and Jack fell to the ground, bleeding out rapidly. Jonathan started pulling himself away from the grisly sight, but he couldn't take his eyes off of it. Josh spun wildly, crying out in shock and swinging his fists every which way. Jack's blood had gotten into his eyes, essentially blinding him, Jonathan realized.

With fiendish speed, the wendigo slashed one unnatural hand, and Josh fell to the ground, his intestines spilling out onto the forest floor. The wendigo reached down and tore something out of Josh and began to eat it. Then it walked forward, stomping on Jake's head, making it pop like an overripe grape. Jonathan was shocked that lives could be taken so easily. One minute here, and the next gone.

Jonathan tried to crawl away faster as Brandon charged, ready to tackle the monster. He was used to it on the football field. No matter how big his opponents, they always went down. Only the monster took the hit and just stood there as though Brandon was a small child. Then, with enormous strength and speed, the wendigo grabbed both of Brandon's wrists and began to lift him to its eye level.

Jonathan, his mouth agape in horror, saw a kicking, screaming Brandon have both his arms pulled so he looked like a person on a cross. Then, with hideous strength, the wendigo pulled Brandon's arms completely out. Blood rushed out in a flood, and the wendigo drank the blood while holding Brandon's now limp body overhead. When the wendigo's thirst was sated, it tossed Brandon's body on top of his friends' lifeless forms.

For the first time, Jonathan saw what looked like an old wound rapidly healing on the creature's calf. As he noticed this, he also saw his knife just in front of it. The wendigo crouched to spring, its hate-filled gaze tearing into Jonathan's soul. He wanted to cry out or beg, but nothing would come out.

Suddenly, Trevor's bat struck the wendigo hard in the back of the head. It didn't go down; it barely moved. "Get away from him, you bitch!" screamed Trevor, getting ready to swing for a home run.

The monster turned to face Trevor and promptly got a face full of bear spray as Cory added, "Chew on that, skinny!"

Jonathan felt an urge to roll his eyes at the movie references, but the wendigo wheeled back, pulling itself up to its full, towering height. It blinked and rubbed at its face forcefully.

Jonathan leapt to his feet and ran forward, saying, "Save some of him for me!" He baseball slid forward and grabbed his knife from the ground where it lay at the wendigo's feet. Then, with a wild cry, he stabbed at its wounded leg.

The knife tore through the injured calf easily, and the wendigo screamed so loudly that all three boys fell to the ground, holding their ears. The world went silent for a moment, but when Jonathan looked up, the monster was gone, and he could see the red and blue of police lights. Then, Jonathan passed out.

CHAPTER 17

What felt like minutes later, Jonathan awoke in what could only be an interrogation room. A metal desk sat before him with the spot where his head had lain embossed with his drool. The uncomfortable plastic chair he sat in was digging into his backside. He stood up and looked around for a camera, then began wildly waving his arms. "Come on—we've gotta get out of here, or more people are going to die! We've got to do something!" His voice broke on the last part, and he began to cry.

Looking down at himself, he saw someone had tried to clean the blood off him. But his clothes were still badly stained. Jonathan was filled with panic; he had to do something. "Where the hell are my friends!"

At that, the door clicked, and Sheriff Roland stepped into the room, shutting the door again behind him.

"Where are my—" started Jonathan, but Roland slammed one hand down on the table, making Jonathan flinch.

"Sit down and shut up till I ask ya a question!"

He sat down across the table from Jonathan and leaned back, crossing his arms. Jonathan leaned forward and pleaded, "We've got to—"

But Roland cut him off again, saying, "What *you* have to do is answer my questions, or you're not going anywhere!"

That's how it went for fifteen minutes. Jonathan told how he and his friends had gone onto the preserve to find out what was killing people. He told how the wendigo had ripped apart the bullies like they were nothing. Jonathan even told how he and his friends had fought back and the wendigo had fled.

However, Sheriff Roland pounded the table with his fist and commanded, "Stop ya lyin'. You and your friends were covered in the football boys' blood. Now, this ain't no game. Tell the truth and you can go home." He said the last bit as though that was what Jonathan wanted. Yet all he really wanted was to get back out there and find his parents and kill the wendigo. It could not be left to live.

"As far as I can tell, you and your friends are part of this. And if you're keeping something from me, that's obstructing the law. You could also be charged with aiding and abetting the killer."

Jonathan opened his mouth angrily and said with a snarl, "How can you be so bull headed? I'm trying to help here!"

Sheriff Roland leaned forward, eager, but a muscle twitched as he clenched his jaw. "Then give me something, kid."

Just then, there was a rap on the door as if someone was whacking it with a hard stick. Roland's face grew even more red than it already was. "What the hell?" he yelled, getting up and stomping over to open the door. On the other side stood the well-dressed man from earlier that night near the Campbells' house.

The man stood with his hat in one hand and his cane in the other. He was only slightly shorter than average, with light-brown hair going silver at the edges. He looked young, but what lines on his face he did have looked like he smiled a lot. His eyes were bright blue and full of mischief. Jonathan noticed his clothes were still immaculate, especially his purple vest. However, his well-made shoes were smudged with dirt.

"It's you again," blurted Jonathan.

"Yes, it is I, Master Campbell, and it is about time we met officially and not simply in passing." He spoke in a clear British accent and had incredible diction.

Roland, though, rudely inserted himself between them. "Now you show up again! You were the one who showed up at the crime scene, asking a lot of questions. Who the hell are you, and what the hell are you doing back here?!"

"I am Cecil Dee, my good constable, and I am young Master Jonathan's godfather."

"And what in the Sam Hill does that have to do with the price of tea in China! You have no business back here. Go . . . before I make you."

Cecil's words didn't change their tone, but he did raise an eyebrow as he answered, "I also happen to be a solicitor on the other side of the pond." Then his words took on a shocked quality, "Don't tell me, Sheriff Roland, that you are questioning young Master Campbell, a minor, without his parents, guardian, or solicitor present."

A shocked silence filled the room and hallway. Who was Cecil Dee? He had come out of nowhere and now was here and claimed to be Jonathan's godfather?

"Come in, then, and let's keep the circus going," answered Roland. Jonathan could not see the sheriff's face, but from his clenched posture, Jonathan was sure he was scowling. "I'm afraid Master Campbell and I are on our way out. The other minors are already with their parents."

"Now wait a—" began Roland, but he was cut off by footsteps in the hallway and snapped to attention. An older, beer-bellied man stood next to Cecil, and he spoke in a deep, serious voice.

"Do what the man says, Sheriff Roland."

"But Chief, I got them red handed. Literally! I know they know something."

"Leave it alone, Sheriff," said the chief of police, putting heavy emphasis on the "sheriff" part. Sheriff Roland's face fell comically, and he pushed past both Cecil and the chief.

Jonathan got to his feet hesitantly and flashed Cecil an uncertain smile. Cecil returned the smile and gave him a wink. Then, he turned to the chief and said politely, "I will also require the tape." The portly chief gave Cecil a disgusted look, then he jerked the door open to the adjoining room and went inside.

"Who the hell are you, and what do you mean you're my godfather? I've never met you before," questioned Jonathan, trying to keep his voice low.

Cecil grinned. "I mean what I say, my lad. Though I may not be very open with the truth, I do not lie." Then the door opened again, and the chief busted through and roughly handed over a CD of some kind.

"Does it come in Blu-ray?" joked Jonathan, trying to break the thick feelings of resentment at the way he was being treated like a criminal. The chief's lips twitched as though he thought about smiling, but he turned away, walking through the sparsely populated bullpen.

Cecil, however, did laugh. It was a nice laugh, full and unrestrained, as though he did it often and relished it each time. He pointed with his cane and said, "Let's go catch up with the rest of the team."

As they walked, Jonathan asked, "What team, and why is there a freaking wendigo in Hannibal, Missouri?"

Pushing open the glass doors, Cecil answered by gesturing to Jonathan's parents and friends, who were all sitting in the family van. "We'll explain on the way."

As Jonathan slid through the open door, his friends greeted him, grinning in spite of the fact that they both looked worse for wear.

"'Bout time," said Cory.

"We've all been waiting on you. What took you so long?" asked Trevor.

"Sheriff Roland seemed to have a crush on me. Must have been because of the knife. Where is my knife, by the way?"

"I've got it for you right here," said his father, handing it to him.

"Picked it up from the preserve for you."

Jonathan glanced at his parents in the front seat. His mom smiled at him warmly and leaned over to plant a kiss on his cheek as he moved to his seat. His dad smiled too, although Jonathan thought he could also see a pained look on his face. Still, it was his usual smile. "Yes, it's about time Cecil got you out. He must be getting rusty in his old age."

"Aw, you should talk, gimpy. Step on the gas. We've got a wendigo to kill."

Jonathan grinned. It was obvious the two knew each other well. He could see it in their relaxed body language as well as the way they spoke to one another.

"So, is he really my godfather? Why have I never met him?"

"Godfather?" his friends mouthed with questioning looks.

His mother turned in her seat. "Cecil was present at your birth; he was your father's best friend." The way she said this told Jonathan that she disapproved of Cecil for some reason.

Cecil answered with what appeared to be a genuine smile. "*Is* his best friend. Do you think, Barbara, that I stayed away because I wanted to?" At the end, he gave Jonathan a pat on the back and a sad smile.

Jonathan started to ask what he meant, but his father cut him off. "Cecil has a dangerous job. You don't bring the types of dangers he deals with to your friends and their families."

Jonathan saw his father give Cecil a weary smile through the rear-view mirror. His mother gave a sigh and looked out the window.

"So, what is it that you do that is so dangerous?" asked Trevor. Jonathan thought he heard scorn in his friend's voice.

However, Cecil only grinned, answering, "I'm glad you asked. It's about time we got around to telling you all this anyway. With your permission, of course, Adam."

Jonathan's father nodded, his eyes serious. Cecil turned fully to Jonathan and his friends with his expression now grave. "Understand what I tell you must stay within this van. I keep these secrets to protect people. If for any reason you can't keep your traps shut, then you're not with the rest of us. Am I understood?"

Jonathan nodded. At this point, he had to know what his parents were involved in. His friends nodded as well.

Cecil gave a soft smile and began, "I belong to an entity known as GCAC, or Global Containment for Aberrant Creatures. Adam was on my team as my tracker. Barbara was our sniper."

Shocked, Jonathan looked at his parents, especially his mother. Adam continued where Cecil left off, his voice deep and somber, "We left the team when you were born to protect you. And we settled here in Hannibal because we had traveled through here numerous times and always wanted to have our lives here."

"But what do you do, and how does it involve us?" asked Cory.

"You made yourselves involved. Now the creature has Jonathan's scent, it will never stop hunting him, and you don't want to have that monster after you," answered Cecil with a stern look before continuing more calmly, "So, what does the word 'aberrant' mean?"

He'd shot the question at all three boys, but of course it was Cory who answered, "It means diverging from what would be normal."

"Exactly, and for me, that can mean a lot. Everything from what would be termed as supernatural to species dubbed as cryptids."

"But why call them cryptids? Why not just admit some creatures are real?" asked Jonathan.

His father fielded the question, answering, "Multiple reasons. One is to protect a species that would be hunted by the public if they knew they were real. Then there is the whole dilemma that if the government added these species to the endangered list, could you imagine how much it would cost to protect them? Therefore, much better to stay silent and let the majority of people never go looking for something like a bigfoot."

Jonathan nodded, then stopped, struck by something his father had said. "Wait, bigfoot is real?" he exclaimed. His father and Cecil nodded. Both bore similar grins of satisfaction.

"Of course, the statistics say that even in our own world, the chances of humans being the only hominid to survive the ice age are simply not probable," said Cecil in a tone much like Cory would use. Jonathan glared at both men.

"Plus, I, your mother, and especially Cecil have often met them," stated his father smugly.

"This has to be a joke, right? I mean cryptids . . . sure. The world is big. But the supernatural?" asked Cory skeptically.

Cecil turned to look at Cory as Adam parked the van outside a storage locker. "You have seen proof of that tonight. Adam can explain while I help Barbara load up. Trevor, you seem to be adjusting well to the news. Lend a hand, lad."

Without complaint, Trevor followed Cecil and Jonathan's mother to the door, which she quickly unlocked. The other three got out of the van, too, and the two boys congregated around Jonathan's father, who was holding his ribs.

"You okay, Dad?" asked Jonathan. He was mad at his parents for keeping secrets, but they were still his parents.

"I'm just milking it," Adam said, giving them a wink.

Not to be put off the subject, Cory asked, "What did he mean— about the proof?"

Adam sighed, leaning against the closed driver's-side door. "To put it easily for you, the wendigo is a demonic spirit. It pushes you during times of starvation and hardship to commit the act of cannibalism. Once the person eats human flesh, the spirit takes over and changes them." He broke off, looking over to a wooded area, his eyes sharp.

Jonathan turned to look in the same direction, but all he saw was a flicker of movement high in the sky, flying away. "Must be an owl," he surmised, shrugging.

But his father's eyes narrowed further.

"You need some good night-vision binoculars. I'll put them on your Christmas list for you," quipped Jonathan. He hoped to break his father out of this apparently introspective mood. However, Adam's eyes only continued to scan the woods, and he took a deep breath through his nose as the wind blew in their direction. *He's sniffing the air*, thought Jonathan.

However, before Jonathan could do the same, his father snapped into motion, grabbing both him and Cory under their arms. "Come on—move!" Adam half shouted. The boys went along with him, hurtling to the storage garage, which was lit by two large overhead fluorescent lamps. His ribs were apparently forgotten. Cecil ran over to Jonathan's father, and the two put their heads together, whispering quickly.

"Jonathan, Cory, come help us out," said Barbara in a loud voice, breaking in on Jonathan's stunned thoughts about what the heck had just happened.

She stood at a folding table with her back to the room. She and Trevor were loading cartridges. As Jonathan got closer, he saw four belts to hold the cartridges for speed loading. One belt was for some type of revolver, he figured, because the bullets looked very large. And on one end of the belt was a large Bowie knife.

"Cory, you can help by loading that empty belt with shotgun shells," Barbara said, pointing to what Jonathan thought must be for his father's gun because a large tomahawk hung through a loop. A third belt was loaded with the thick magazines for his mother's rifle. The final belt being worked on by his mother had pistol cartridges of what looked like nine-millimeter bullets. That is, if you compared the revolver bullets to the magazine's size. There was also an empty loop for a knife on one side and a holster on the other for a pistol.

Barbara's eyes met Jonathan's, and she smiled wanly, motioning for him to follow her. She led him to a line of shelves where several large metal cases sat along with one new-looking plastic case. Taking the plastic case down with shaking hands, she motioned for Jonathan to position himself on the floor with her. The case was upside down, so Jonathan couldn't see what brand it contained, but he thought it must be some sort of pistol.

Without pause, Barbara started, her eyes boring holes into the case. "Your father had his gift to give to you for your protection, and I wanted to give you something of mine. I may not have a knife with ancient historical significance, but I've always been good with guns." Then, she turned the case over, revealing steel letters that read *Sig Sauer*. Jonathan felt his heart beating nearly as fast as it had when he'd received his knife. His eyes met his mother's, and she gave a bittersweet smile in response to the excitement that must have shown on Jonathan's face.

Finally, she opened the case to show a brand-new gun, matte black in color, with a night sight already attached. "This is a P320, the full-size version to fit your hands better. It's a Luger, of course, like all Sig Sauers."

"What's it made of?" asked Jonathan, gingerly picking the gun up. It was light, and just like she said, it fit well in his large hand. Pointing it down and away from them, Jonathan turned the gun to the side to look at it, loving the weapon's sleek finish.

"It's stainless steel and carbon steel. And the grip is a standard polymer, which makes it lightweight," she rattled off like some kind of gun thesaurus.

"And it takes nine-millimeter bullets, right?" asked Jonathan, pulling back the slide smoothly and seeing it was clean and well oiled.

His mother nodded, saying, "It has a magazine capacity of seventeen rounds, which is two more than the compact version."

"Wow! I always knew you were knowledgeable about guns, but you're like—an expert!" said Jonathan, finally looking up at her.

To his surprise, tears ran slowly down her cheeks as she said softly, "I never wanted this life for you, hun."

He didn't know what to do. So he placed the gun back in the case and hugged her.

"Thank you," he whispered.

Her response was a contented hum of approval. Then at last they broke, and Jonathan wiped his eyes.

"We've got to get you ready," she said and held out the belt.

Jonathan put it on, sliding his knife into its place on his left side. The gun—his gun—went on his right hip. Jonathan pulled it out and made sure the safety was on. His mother showed him how to load it quickly. He did it a few times, getting used to the motion because he might have to do it in the dark.

Then he smiled. "Thank you, Mom. If I'm being honest, I kept feeling helpless with the wendigo after me. But now, I have another way to defend myself."

She smiled in return, but her eyes remained troubled. "I'm sorry for that. If we had successfully killed it, then you wouldn't have to help us. However, we don't think it is your normal, run-of-the-mill wendigo."

"Okay, you're going to have to explain. What happened? How did Dad get hurt? Also, what the heck do you mean by 'not a normal wendigo'? I thought it was bad enough just having a wendigo at all."

Jonathan's father spoke from behind him, making him jump. "I got rusty. Like we said, your mother and I have not hunted since you were born."

Jonathan turned to him. "Just tell me what happened; I'm not a baby."

His father answered with a grin, saying, "We know you're not." And then to his wife, "I'm glad you gave him the gun. Better to be prepared than hiding from something that will always find you." He smiled lovingly at her, and they gave each other a quick kiss.

Then, he turned back to Jonathan, all business. "Cecil came to us today, hoping we had a rifle for him to use. We of course gave him the keys to this storage garage to stock up for a hunt. He said he had found evidence that the perpetrator of the attack last night was a wendigo."

"How did he get here so quickly?" asked Jonathan, glancing over at Cecil, who was now checking what looked like two revolvers while telling Jonathan's friends an apparently hilarious story.

Jonathan's father continued, "Cecil was in the area. Why he was is his business. The local police apparently gave him some trouble about getting in to find the wendigo. Monsters don't exactly sit still and let you hunt them."

Jonathan nodded, "So that's why he was so happy to see Sheriff Roland upset."

His parents both laughed, and some of the tension he had felt from them eased. "Cecil has never been good with local police," said his mother with a chuckle.

Adam laughed, saying, "Because of their interference, it took time to track the wendigo down. When he finally did, it was outside our house."

"I saw its eyes," Jonathan said, shivering at the memory of the green orbs staring back at him with pure hatred. "I wasn't sure what it was. And then I thought I heard a car backfire in the distance."

Adam nodded gravely. "That was Cecil. But the wendigo managed to dodge the shot, so it only took a flesh wound." Something about the story didn't sound right to Jonathan, but he didn't say anything. Unaware that he had said something wrong, his father doggedly continued, "When he missed his shot and realized it must be after you, he called us out of retirement. We were not ready for it," he said sadly.

His mother continued the account, "Cecil is not a great tracker, but a blood trail is easy to follow. We got together at a house on the southeast edge of town and found the inhabitants dead. It was awful," she finished simply.

"I tracked the carnage," Adam added. "It was a trap, though; the damn creature hit me from behind. We all barely got away, and only because my tomahawk injured it. And your mother put it through a wall with a shot." He gave his wife a side hug, and she hugged him back. "I've never seen a creature heal as fast as that one does. We are talking seconds, not minutes. There is something weird about this wendigo."

Jonathan frowned. "What do you mean? I thought all creatures like the wendigo, vampires, and werewolves heal fast."

"You're right, son, but healing fast is different than what that wendigo can do. When a supernatural creature is hurt by a weapon of faith like your knife or my tomahawk, it normally takes time to heal. Usually, it takes a feeding session to heal such injuries. However, even though I hurt its leg with my weapon, it still got to you, and the boys said its leg injury looked like a week-old wound."

"Well, you apparently know this stuff better than me. So, what does this all mean?" Jonathan couldn't help it. He'd been into this type of stuff for years, but his parents had never alluded to knowing anything about it. He felt like he had been lied to his whole life. What were they not telling him right now?

"It means, as your father said, this wendigo is not normal," stated his mother, her eyes on Cecil, who was waving them over. There was a hard, protracted silence between them.

Finally, his father stepped forward. "Listen, I promise I'll tell you everything I know when we are done with this bloody business. I have one more gift for you at home." He turned Jonathan around, and they began to walk towards Cecil. Then, bending next to Jonathan's ear, he whispered, "If I don't make it through this, look under the pool table. On top of the leg furthest from the basement stairs, you will find a hollow. Inside is a book for you with everything I know."

Jonathan looked at his father, startled. He certainly wanted his father to make it through alive. But he also wanted to know what was in that book, information that had been hidden from him.

CHAPTER 18

Once at the table, Jonathan sat down in a folding chair his friends had procured. Everyone was sitting except for Cecil, who was holding a manila folder.

Jonathan thought Cecil looked like King Arthur as he stood at one end of the table. Except that this table was square. Looking at everyone in turn, deliberately he said, "When dealing with the supernatural, knowledge is our best weapon." He slapped the manila folder down with a flourish.

"So, is that your information?" asked Cory.

Cecil nodded sharply, saying, "Before I begin, why don't you, Adam, tell us how a wendigo is created, just so we are all on the same page."

Jonathan's father cleared his throat very importantly, then began, "The dark spirit known by many as the wendigo pushes a person to commit narcissistic acts of cannibalism. Once he commits the act, he changes into the wendigo with a kind of . . . what would best be described as a possession."

"Okay, but how is it different from the sailors who were lost at sea who committed cannibalism?" broke in Cory.

Jonathan's father grinned at Cory and replied, "You're right to correlate the two things, but it has to do with how the act was done. In the case of the sailors, lots were drawn. Or the first to die was eaten. In other words, one could argue no spirit was pushing them. The choice wasn't made with selfishness. However, many argue that in the case of the Donner party, where someone selfishly killed others and ate them to survive, the key is that the person made a choice that another's life was less important than theirs."

Cecil clapped his hands together once, making the three friends jump. Then he said, "That is exactly what I mean. With that knowledge, I was able to narrow down who the wendigo was!"

"So, who is it?" asked Barbara.

Cecil flipped open the folder and pulled out a scan of a newspaper. "It's David Cabe, the foreman!"

Jonathan leaned in to read the paper. It was a report of a cave-in on July sixth of nineteen sixty. During an attempt to chisel out more rock, there was a cave-in, and seven men, including David Cabe, were trapped. The blame for the cave-in fell on the foreman, who had been pushing his people on twelve-hour workdays to match a quota.

"Okay, then what happened next?" asked Jonathan.

Cecil frowned at the question, and he pulled out another news report and numerous posters of missing persons. Jonathan read through the report that stated trespassers in the mine were found dead. Apparently, some surviving crew members attempted, a month later, to finally rescue those who were missing. Why they had waited so long, Jonathan couldn't begin to guess. Maybe because they thought their friends were already dead or they were greedy to get at what Cabe had been trying to reach.

Either way, the trespassers were found torn apart, and all that was left of the missing miners was scattered bones. There was no way to guess who the bones belonged to. Cecil broke in on Jonathan's reading, "One can surmise that Cabe killed and ate these trespassers and went on a rampage. Which is why ten people went missing in Hannibal." They all nodded in horror at the thought of the whole disgusting event.

"But then, how is Cabe—the wendigo—back? And what's he been doing for the last sixty years?" asked Cory, voicing Jonathan's curiosity as well.

Jonathan saw Cecil and his father share a look. Then, his father said, "We retired here for a reason other than what I told you. We don't know exactly what happened. What we do know is what your grandfather told me. He was placed here by the GCAC to keep watch for the wendigo to reemerge. Your grandfather said by the time an investigator got here, the wendigo had disappeared. But we have a good idea where it went, thanks to Cecil."

"And where's that?" growled Jonathan. He was seriously getting fed up with all these secrets and lies.

His mother spoke for the first time during the discussion, and her voice was a whip crack. "Change your tone or you'll stay out of this fight even if I have to tie you up myself and ship you to China!"

Jonathan looked away, grinding his teeth and clenching his hands into fists until he calmed down enough to tune back in. Cecil was in the middle of saying, ". . . since we know Cabe stayed in the cave for a long period of time. Then, it would make sense that he has claimed the land around the caves as his hunting ground."

Suddenly, Trevor spoke up, "If that's true, then why is he after Jonathan?"

Adam answered politely, "It has to do with our blood. Our family has a long history of battling evil, especially the wendigo. All that evil left a kind of stain, letting dangerous creatures know who the hunters are. That's why, when it ambushed us, it went after me first."

"If that's true, why doesn't it go after you, Cecil?" asked Jonathan.

"That's not pertinent right now, so let's focus on the present."

"So, what's the plan, Cecil?" asked Barbara, not looking at him.

Jonathan wondered why she was mad at him, but he decided to ask about it later. "Well, to start, we will have Barb as usual in a sniper position to guard our backs. We are going to lure the creature to the amphitheater, where we will immobilize it and burn it. We are going to need some fuel and some bait."

"My son and husband are not bait," Barbara growled. Adam just frowned, apparently thinking it through.

"Barbara, if we try to set a trap without using bait, there is a good chance it will see the trap and ambush us like it did before," said Cecil, his voice rising.

Jonathan's mother, though she was shorter than almost everyone except Cory, stepped right up to Cecil and got in his face. "No, we find another way," she said, her voice rising in turn.

"There is no better way. That *thing* is a predator! Give it something to hunt, and it will fall into our trap," shouted Cecil.

"Do you have any humanity left, Cec—" started Barbara.

However, Adam barked out, "Enough!" They both turned to him, his face now calm, where for a moment it had looked angry. Barbara's face was beet red from her own anger, but Cecil had quickly pacified himself and looked a little sad. Jonathan wondered what his mother was going to say and if it meant anything. Focusing instead on his father, he stored the information away.

"Barbara, his idea makes sense. The wendigo wants me and Jonathan. So let's use that," said his father. His mother huffed, saying nothing, but turned away to look over their supplies.

Trevor walked over to a rack of equipment and brought down two machetes. "Cory and I will use these. It will do us better than some baseball bats."

Cory, raising a hand like he was in class, asked, "What will we use as fuel?"

Without thinking, Cecil answered, "Diesel fuel burns longer and slower due to its longer carbon chain."

Cory blinked at Cecil and asked, "How do you know all of this?"

At that, both Cecil and Adam broke out into laughter. After a minute of this, Jonathan could have sworn he heard his mother giggle a little.

Finally, when the laughter subsided, Cecil answered, "It's all experience over time. When you make enough mistakes, you start to learn."

Jonathan picked up two gas tanks from a shelf of car equipment. "Well then, let's fill these up and get started."

"I couldn't agree more," said his father, smacking him on the back.

As they all walked to the door, his mother hugged Jonathan with one arm, and he felt his face heat with embarrassment. In fact, when he finished the hug and managed to pull himself away, Cory gave him a shoulder bump, which Jonathan returned with interest.

As Cory came to bump Jonathan again with a huge grin on his face, Trevor came out of nowhere and bumped them both. "Enough, you two idiots. Let's get our game faces on," he said as the doors rolled open.

Jonathan rolled his eyes, and Cory shot him the finger. Then they heard Adam curse. Next to the car stood Sheriff Roland, his hand on his gun.

CHAPTER 19

Adam gulped. They were all brimming with weapons. Whatever Cecil had told the police chief, Roland was ignoring it. "I don't care who you are. You're gettin' the hell out of my town," roared Roland.

Adam stepped forward, putting a hand up, and said, "Sheriff, we are only trying to help." However, as he stepped forward, Roland was so jumpy that he half drew his gun as though Adam's movement had been a threat.

"Just stay where you are. Everyone, disarm and lie down face first." Though he still appeared all gruff and angry, Adam could see his left hand shaking slightly. Adam's words were not getting through to him. Then, Cecil blew out a breath of irritation, and Adam knew what was coming. Adam had seen how Cecil handled tough situations when diplomacy had failed. It was time for some tough love, so Adam readied himself to run forward.

Adam glanced at Cecil out of the corner of his eye. He stood in the classic, two-handed Weaver stance, primed and ready. Doing his best to distract Roland, Adam took another deliberate step forward. Just as planned, Roland fully raised his gun, and in the time the gun was pointed away from the boys, Cecil fired. Roland's gun was shot from his grip. Wringing his hands, Roland turned to find his gun, which had landed under the van.

Adam ran forward, ignoring the pain in his ribs, and hit Roland hard in the temple with a right cross. Roland crumpled to the ground, unconscious.

"Jesus! Have you done that before?" asked Jonathan.

His father was grinning widely. "Only when I need to."

Adam bent and with a grunt of effort lifted Roland into a fireman's carry. Wincing at the stabbing pain in his torso, he made his way back inside the storage garage. "Someone help me get him inside," he barked, expecting the three boys to still be back by Cecil, mouths agape like gasping fish.

However, when he looked around, all three were following like the curious children they still were. He grinned at them although he still felt the burning pain coming from his ribs. He didn't want Jonathan or Barbara to know how much pain he was in, so he did his best to conceal it with his pride for the boys, especially his own, who returned the grin, apparently still nervous.

Adam understood it wasn't every day you saw your father knock out an officer of the law. "Help me with him," said Adam once inside the storage garage. Jonathan and Trevor both grabbed the officer and lowered him to the ground. Adam grinned; he was going to enjoy this part. Though they were far removed from the atrocities of the past, some wounds ran deep. Also, Roland, who had been overheard in town saying, "An Indian ain't a true American," had always given Adam a hard time and even hindered his business. The sheriff often parked outside the Campbells' store like he needed to be there for some reason. And when potential customers saw a law enforcement vehicle there, they would often just leave and go somewhere else.

"Now, sit him up. There should be some cuffs in the back of his belt." Cory, being the son of a lawyer, stood back, his mouth hanging open at what they were doing to a law enforcement officer. Adam grinned at the boy and explained, "We are doing this to keep him out of harm's way."

"Still, this breaks a bunch of laws. My dad is going to be so mad," he answered.

Adam nodded seriously, but knowing the kind of relationship Cory had with his parents, he answered, "Oh, he is going to be pissed." Cory grinned and stepped forward to help.

Adam laughed and turned away to let the boys finish handcuffing Roland. Cecil was collecting Roland's gun while Barbara passionately but quietly argued with him. Adam frowned; he understood how his wife felt, but still—this was life and death. If the wendigo was allowed to live, it would never stop hunting Jonathan until he was dead and gone. Adam would not let that happen!

Looking to make sure the boys were still busy with Roland, Adam briskly walked over to the arguing pair. "Enough, both of you! We can't stand divided! We must come together or be broken alone. Barbara, we have to do this. We cannot let Cecil fight it alone. And Cecil, ease up on my wife and have some empathy."

Cecil took off his hat and gave a short bow to them. Then, putting his hat back on, he said in a loud voice, "Okay, boys, hop to it."

All three boys hurried over, putting their weapons and gas cans in the back of the van. Jonathan slammed the cargo doors closed and turned to Adam and Cecil, who grinned. Adam did his best to match the smile. The excitement of the hunt had taken over Cecil. Adam felt the stirrings of it in himself, as well. He heard Barbara open the passenger door and knew she was getting in and placing her rifle in its normal spot on the floor.

"Let's get this thing," said Adam, walking over to his own door. He stopped when he heard soft footsteps behind him. Adam swirled around, expecting to see the wendigo about to leap on him. However, it was only Jonathan. He looked wide eyed at Adam's sudden turn. Adam smiled at his son, doing his best to calm his fast-beating heart. "What's up, bud?" he asked, trying to not let show how rattled he was. Adam had barely heard his own son's approach.

"I just wanted to let you know that it means a lot to me. You know—letting me do this."

Adam hugged his son and whispered in his ear, "If I had my way I'd agree with your mother. But sadly, during times like these, sometimes the best choice is the one we don't like. Remember that sometimes we have to make tough decisions that we detest."

His son hugged him back tightly. "Still . . . thanks, Dad."

Somewhere far off, an owl hooted, and the two broke apart as though the call of the night bird had signaled something. The moment was over, and Jonathan opened the door and got into the middle seat, joining Cecil. The other two boys were already talking to Jonathan from where they sat in the back seat. Adam got in himself and started the trusty van. As he pulled out of the gate of the storage facility, he felt his wife's hand on his leg. Adam looked at her and smiled.

They were a pair, both in hunting and as lovers. As long as they were together, they could overcome any obstacles. Driving in the direction of a QuikTrip gas station, Adam said, "Okay, Cecil, update everyone on how you kill a wendigo. Then, go over your plan."

With a flourish of his hand, Cecil turned slightly in his chair so that he was talking to the whole car and not excluding the boys in the seat behind him. "A wendigo is nigh immortal. Though it is pushed to forever feed on and hunt humans, it cannot be killed by its endless starvation. It does not die of old age, and this one especially heals as quickly as almost any other supernatural creature."

"But why is this one so special and different?" interrupted Jonathan. The other two boys agreed.

"We can experiment and figure out that mystery once the wendigo is dead and gone," said Cecil, striking his own leg for emphasis. Then, he continued more calmly, "It cannot be allowed that this wendigo continues to exist. I do agree that we need to know what is unique about it.

However, we don't need to know what makes it different until it's dead."

"Can I ask why?" asked Trevor unsurely.

Cecil sighed, "Because both Adam's and Jonathan's weapons proved that although it does heal faster, the effect of faith weapons is still the same—they cause worse injury than the standard weapons. So, if it still obeys the same supernatural rules, then what is the difference?" He shot this question at the boys like a classroom teacher to his students.

Jonathan had followed the line of thought. "Whatever is different is on the biological side. Therefore, it can be killed by the normal supernatural ways." Adam smiled at his son in the mirror, and Barbara took one of Adam's hands. Her hand shook slightly, and Adam gripped it more tightly to reassure her.

Cory asked, his voice sounding irritated, "But what are these normal ways to kill a wendigo?"

Cecil nodded, then began, "Normally, you kill a wendigo by first subduing it with weapons such as guns, knives, and our faith weapons. The wendigo during this stage may look and act dead, but what is happening is you have pushed the spirit possessing the individual to focus purely on healing and not on animating the individual. The individual is not dead, but they have no will of their own, so this time is critical. While it's down, you burn it to ashes, especially the heart."

"Why is the heart so important if it's a supernatural creature and not a cryptid?" asked Jonathan.

At this, Adam spoke up, "A wendigo is still a spirit of winter. No matter where the wendigo exists, that doesn't change. That's why they carry the cold and death with them. Also, their hearts are made of ice. Look at this frozen heart as the connection to the spirit. Once that is done, both host and spirit are banished."

"Isn't there anything we could do for the host?" asked the kind-hearted Trevor.

All three adults shook their heads, but as he knew the wendigo best,

Adam answered, "No, Trevor. Many people have tried. However, when a person reaches the stage of possession where they have committed the act of cannibalism, there is no going back."

In a show of support, Cory slapped Trevor on the back, and Jonathan gave him a hand, which Trevor smacked, smiling. It was heartening to see how the boys encouraged one another.

As Adam pulled up to the QuikTrip pumps, there was a cacophony of seat belts being undone. Putting the van into park, Adam shot a look back at the boys.

"Got to have energy for tonight, Dad." With that, Jonathan led his friends inside to get snacks and unhealthy amounts of caffeine. The adults all gave a chuckle. It was a little refreshing to have the boys with them. Still, all three were on high alert for the reappearance of the wendigo.

Adam got out of the van, slid his credit card, and began putting gas into the tanks. Then, the hair on his arms stood on end as a blast of cold air stole over him. Adam jumped and reached for his shotgun, but a hand grabbed him and pulled him upright. Whirling around, expecting to die, Adam found it was Cecil. As with Jonathan, he had not heard his friend's approach.

This fact disturbed him, so he looked around wildly for the danger.

Cecil pointed out into the night. "I think it is in or was in that house over there."

The house in question was directly across the street; it was a small, single-story, powder-blue structure. The fence around it was so white it seemed to glow in the moonlight. Distinct on the center of the fence facing them was the arterial spray of blood where someone had been torn apart and dragged over the top of it.

There was the click-clack sound of a shotgun, and Adam looked around to see Barbara with his weapon in hand and her own rifle over one shoulder. He hurriedly took his gun and popped the safety, then looked around more carefully. Out of the corner of his eye, he saw Cecil draw one of his Webleys and check the bullets with a quick flick of the break. Then, with a snap, he flicked it back and asked calmly, "Do you have it, Barb?"

As a sniper, and with a thermal-vision scope, this was all hers until they were close to the wendigo. For almost a full minute, Adam and Cecil turned this way and that, during which Adam's senses were going crazy, every small sound drawing his attention. It was like hunting a ghost.

Barbara let out a slow breath and spoke calmly, "I've got a heat signature." Adam looked at her and followed her gaze to a house across the street from the little blue house.

"Do you have a shot?" asked Cecil calmly.

"No," she answered. Then, after a pause, she actually cursed. "It's the neighbor." Her rifle swung left and right looking for a trail.

"It might be a trap," said Cecil, drawing his second gun. He quickly checked the weapon, then took a step in the direction of the house.

"We've got to hunt *it*, not let it hunt *us*. It's turning this night against us," growled Adam. Then, from behind them, there was a splatting sound. Adam and the others spun around to find a human arm lying in the light of the deserted gas station.

"It's on top of the building," said Cecil. He sounded calm, his guns still ready but now at his sides.

Then Adam understood it was the gas, and hurriedly putting the full tanks in the van, he whispered to Barbara, "Hurry and get the kids. We have your back."

She nodded, her eyes wide with fear, but she understood that the monster had them and could take them at any moment. Therefore, acting scared with sudden movements and a lot of noise could spell fear, and fearful prey was good prey to a wendigo.

Putting her gun in the van, she speed-walked to the gas station doors, pushed through them, and went inside. Adam could see Barbara saying something, motioning furiously at the boys, their hands full of items. Adam thought he heard scrabbling on the roof, and he pointed his shotgun above the doors of the building.

Cecil put his back to Adam's to cover the other side of the roof. "This is like old times, huh?" said Cecil.

Adam let out a pent-up breath and answered, "Kind of like Africa, yeah. It feels like we are always on the back foot with both cases."

"You remember that case too, huh? Yeah, the Blemmyes are not something to mess with. Our intelligence was apparently wrong about the numbers."

"That's a bit of an understatement; there were over a hundred of those. In any case, I know you have a team. Where the hell are they?"

Adam, whose eyes were on the ceiling when he spoke, tore them away to Barbara, who was apparently calmly paying the obviously high teen behind the counter. Then he flicked his eyes back to the roof, where the wendigo's head appeared. It met his eyes, and Adam took the shot. The wendigo was so fast, though, that the shot just grazed it. Still, Adam heard it growl and rapidly move around to another side of the roof. This had to be a trick, thought Adam, so he kept his eyes on the side closest to him.

Cecil was a pro; he had his side covered. "They are in Chicago dealing with their own situation with a small werewolf problem."

Just then, Barbara and the boys burst through the doors and ran for the van. Adam kept his gaze on the roof, yelling, "We got your backs! Get in the van; move it, boys."

The boys, especially his son with his long legs, ran the distance in seconds. Then, they were in the van, and it was just Adam and Cecil outside the vehicle. There was another scratching sound from the roof before the wendigo leapt into view on the right side of the gas station's building. Cecil shot it twice before it took a step, one shot in each shoulder. Then, Adam caught it full in the stomach, throwing the wendigo back into the darkness. Not waiting to see the monster get back to its feet,

Adam and Cecil jumped back into the van and slammed the doors shut.

Adam hit the gas with a scream of tires and peeled off into the night. They had gone a hundred feet or so when something massive hit the roof. Adam reached for his shotgun from the floorboards at his side, but Barbara beat him to it. She pulled on the trigger, and thunder filled the van. Adam couldn't tell if she'd hit her target, but he slammed on the brakes. There was a screech of nails as the wendigo was thrown from the roof. Not wasting a second, Adam stomped on the gas again and drove over the prone wendigo.

There was a distinct thump as the tires bumped over it. Then Barbara cried out as a claw went straight through her door to score her leg. Adam jerked the steering wheel from side to side to throw it off. He didn't know what to do as a second hand pierced the sliding door. Then, with a cry, Jonathan leapt forward and slashed at the inhuman hand at his door, taking off two elongated fingers. Both hands released the doors, and there was another thump as the back tires went over the wendigo.

"You all right, Mom?" asked Jonathan.

Barbara grimaced, but Adam thought only he saw it as she answered, "Just a scratch. Cecil, do you have anything—"

Before she could finish, he handed up gauze and medical tape. "You sure you're all right?" he asked, meeting Barbara's eyes for a moment.

Barbara nodded, and Adam put out a comforting hand that she squeezed in return.

"Now, do we all see why we cannot leave this wendigo alive?" asked Cecil, his voice directed at the boys. Looking in the rearview mirror, he saw the boys all answer with nods.

Jonathan's face was full of concern for his mother. Finally, he asked, "The claws aren't poisoned or something like that, right?"

He'd asked this question to the van at large, but it was Cecil who answered, "No, nothing like that. She may have a wound, like if a cat scratched you. However, the wendigo does not turn you into one of its own as would happen with other supernatural creatures."

Jonathan nodded, still looking worried, but his shoulders relaxed. However, Cecil was in teaching mode as he continued, unperturbed, "You see, it makes sense if you think about it. For instance, things such as vampires and werewolves are often concerned with spreading their affliction. However, the wendigo likes solitude. Though there may be more wendigos in the world, they prefer space between their territories, much like certain cat species, like the mountain lion or jaguar."

"It makes sense, but can we use the natural world to explain the supernatural world?" asked Cory.

"Of course," answered Jonathan automatically before Cecil added, smiling, "Yes, our young friend is correct. Though the supernatural world goes to extremes, when it comes to nature, it does not and cannot go outside the bounds of physics."

Cory nodded his understanding and looked out the window.

"Okay, you say that this supernatural world obeys the laws of physics. Well, what does that mean when it comes to something like ghosts? How can that obey the laws of physics?" asked Trevor, interested and actually leaning forward in his seat. Adam could see Jonathan and Trevor were both eager to learn, while Cory was still having a tough time admitting such things that he believed were just theory could be real.

Adam could remember his own skepticism when his father and Cecil had told him about how the world really was. He answered Trevor's question just as they had told him all those years ago, "Spirits and ghosts and even our souls are made up of energy. Though we don't know much about this energy, suffice it to say that the energy that they produce to live and affect the world around them is not taken from nothing. As you learn in high school physics, energy can be changed. However, it is not made from nothing. Also, it cannot be destroyed. Therefore, it follows the laws of physics. Just because we don't understand something, it doesn't make it untrue."

"What about the cryptids? Do they all exist then?" asked Jonathan eagerly.

Adam, Barbara, and Cecil all laughed at his eagerness. His zeal for knowledge reminded them of how Cecil always was and indeed how Adam had been at Jonathan's age. It was Cecil who answered, "All? Well, I don't know about all. The world is wide, but if you come with me and learn from me, you will be amazed at what you find."

"I think we have enough going on without thinking about all that," said Barbara sharply. Just then, they pulled into the parking lot at Sodalis Nature Preserve, and Adam stopped the vehicle dead. Several cars were already there, including a jeep with a plethora of bumper stickers . . . all covered in blood. Out in a field, there were some lamps that lit up the site of what looked like a massacre.

In a large torn-up net were two bodies. They looked like they had gotten tangled in the net and butchered. The bodies of the teens from the biological group were gone, but their blood still stained the grass and amphitheater. "Blast it," swore Cecil, and he opened the door and ran to the bodies in the nets to see if they could do anything to save them.

Adam grabbed his shotgun and streaked after Cecil, who was pulling out his Webley. Jonathan was at Adam's side, and he was glad to have inherited his father's long legs. And he was glad they could stop the others from seeing the carnage that waited for them.

Both of the victims' heads had been ripped off and placed purposely so they looked towards those approaching from the parking lot. One was that of what might have been a young, plump, pretty woman with red hair. The other was a young adult male with dark hair and eyes. His broken glasses had actually been placed back on his head as though to help him see again. The bodies, though, were not so distinct. They had been torn apart, with pieces strewn in all directions. It was hard to say which body part belonged to which person.

Jonathan promptly threw up and began to choke with sobs.

Adam tried to console him and prevent the others from seeing what had happened here. The deaths of these adults were meant to make a statement. Even as he tried to calm Jonathan, he looked over the ground to try and figure out what had happened.

They had not been killed at the Jeep, merely subdued, though he thought from the blood in an unnecessarily violent way. The victims had then been dragged to this net, where they had been butchered. According to the torn-up ground, both had been alive during at least part of the savagery.

Adam looked over at Cecil, who was slowly and methodically loading his guns. Meeting Cecil's eyes, he asked, "You got the same thing I did, then?"

"What did you get?" asked Jonathan, breathing hard. "What could this possibly mean?" he demanded, his voice rising to a shout.

Cecil, walking calmly over so that he stood between the others and the bodies, answered, "It means it's ready for us. It knows we mean to trap it. And it's giving us the message that if we do, it will tear us all apart just the same." Then, very pointedly, he began removing his dapper vest and his hat. He was going in all business. Cecil was done with chasing the wendigo; this hunt would end here.

CHAPTER 20

Jonathan stared at Cecil as he calmly handed his clothes and cane to Trevor, who dutifully took them back to the van.

"Bring all the gear, too. Cory, you help him. Barbara, move into position," Cecil instructed. Only after Cory ran off and Barbara moved off with her rifle did Cecil turn back to Jonathan and Adam. He looked at them both, his blue eyes boring into them. Cecil's whole demeanor had changed; he was suddenly commanding and stern. His usual kindly smile was gone, and he seemed to glow with authority.

"What do we—" Jonathan started to say, but his father cut him off with a gesture.

Jonathan stayed quiet as Cecil in a strangely calm voice said, "You two are our only chance to make this work. It knows this is a trap, but if it wants you two as badly as I think it does, we still have a shot at this. Make it chase you, make it want you, then get your asses back here, and we will kill it and burn it. Then, we will find who is behind this." At these final words, Jonathan thought he heard Cecil's gun groan in protest at his white-knuckled grip.

Jonathan nodded. He couldn't think what else he could do. He was in this fight, and despite feeling small and wanting to run and hide like a frightened rabbit, he knew he had to stand his ground and pull his weight. His hands at his sides, he felt the gun and knife there. How had things changed so fast? From an interested person on the sidelines to being in the middle of a nightmare.

Then his father's voice broke through his brain fog. "Shake it off, Jonathan. If you pause and freeze up, one or both of us will end up dead."

"Right. Just tell me what to do."

"Just follow my lead, and if I say run, you run back the way we came and don't look back."

Jonathan looked at his father, troubled. "But what if . . . " Jonathan began, but his father stopped him.

"Enough. You either do as I say, or I lock you in the van and I do this alone," he growled.

"All right," Jonathan agreed, hating himself for agreeing to run even if it meant the death of his father. He felt like the chicken all the bullies thought he was.

However, as he pushed aside low-hanging branches, he knew he couldn't change his father's mind. Instead, Jonathan did his best to stay close and be as quiet as possible.

"I do want you to know, Jonathan, that I am proud of you."

"What do you mean?" the boy whispered back.

"You rallied your friends, and you fought off the wendigo when it was bearing down on you. I couldn't have done any better."

Jonathan felt himself bubble up with warmth and pride in himself. Had he really done all that in one night? "I didn't do this stuff alone, though," he acknowledged, shoving aside a sap-covered fir branch. Needles fell like rain to the dark ground that crunched underfoot in spite of Jonathan doing his best to not make a sound.

"No one sane does this type of thing alone," Adam stated.

"What about Cecil? Wasn't he hunting the wendigo on his own?"

"For one thing, I never said Cecil was completely sane. And for another, his investigation was on his own while figuring out what he was hunting. Ill advised, but technically not crazy." They both chuckled softly, and then, all of a sudden, Jonathan felt it. There was a bone-chilling cold coming over him. Even the ground was slightly frosted. "It is getting stronger the longer it is out and killing," said his father tersely. "Get ready."

Adam pulled out his tomahawk. Jonathan pulled out his own gun with a shaking hand. However, for some reason, when he took the knife in the other hand, his shaking calmed. The knife in his dominant hand somehow made him feel braver. Suddenly, with the speed of thought, the enormous wendigo dropped from above. Since it was directly over him, Jonathan slashed at whatever he could reach. He finally scored a long cut on its right arm but was backhanded aside for his efforts.

Jonathan's head hit the cold, hard ground, and his breath went out with a huff. Through his spinning vision, he saw his father bury his tomahawk in the wendigo's side, right into the creature's sickeningly prominent ribcage. Jonathan didn't even see what happened next, but with a cry of pain, his father was sent flying into the darkness behind Jonathan.

Jonathan looked to see where his father had landed, but his eyes snapped back to the wendigo as it screamed in pain. It had removed the tomahawk from its ribs. It spat blood and grinned a sharp, bloody-toothed smile. "Now you're all mine, meat," said the wendigo in an inhumanly high, piercing voice.

Jonathan, in his desperation, said, "David Cabe, Mr. Cabe, are you still in there?"

The wendigo twitched, and its head turned bird-like to the side as though hearing something it knew but couldn't grasp.

Then, the creature actually laughed so high and cold that Jonathan thought it would freeze his own beating heart. When it spoke again, it said in what must have been David Cabe's voice, "The meat sack is long dead, long dead; there is only I." With that, it began to walk forward, one long-legged step at a time.

Without thinking, Jonathan frantically shot his gun six times, not even aiming. However, since they were so close and the wendigo so large, there was no way he could miss all the shots.

Two shots did, in fact, miss, but the other four hit the wendigo square in the chest. The monster reared back for a moment, and then, as though angered by this, it leapt into the air. Its arms were outstretched towards Jonathan, its mouth of needle-sharp teeth ready to rip out his throat. Jonathan was going to die; he could see it in the wendigo's pitiless green eyes. Then, a roar of sound hit Jonathan, and the wendigo was thrown back to fall into a patch of bushes.

Jonathan sat up and turned to see his father coming out of the darkness, his shotgun at the ready. Without wasting time, Adam pumped a shell, aimed, and fired, throwing the struggling wendigo back down.

"Get the heck out of here, Jonathan! I'll hold it back and then come after you!"

The wendigo snarled and headed for the canopy of the trees, probably to get out of range and get another sneak attack. However, it was caught again in midair by Adam's shotgun shell, and the wendigo flew backwards, slamming into the tree."

Jonathan turned back to his father, uncertain. He only had three shots left, and Jonathan couldn't just leave him. "I said *go!*" yelled his father. Jonathan winced and hurried past him into the darkness, feeling like the most worthless person in the world.

All at once, resolve stole over Jonathan, and he ran as fast as he could. If his father wanted him to run, then he would outrun the wind itself. He gasped for breath, and small twigs scratched him in his passing, but he couldn't stop. Two more shots from his father's gun went off in quick succession. Dimly, Jonathan was aware of tears streaming down his scratched and bleeding face.

There was a long pause where the only thing Jonathan heard was his own footfalls, the breaking of small branches, and his own heavy breathing. Finally, a sixth shot rang out, and there was an anguished cry of pain. A long pause followed; then came a scream of fury from the wendigo. It had killed his father and was coming for him now.

Jonathan did not know he could run faster, but he poured on the speed until he burst into the clearing. Looking around wildly, he saw only Cecil in some type of shooter stance, gun up and ready. He hardly looked like the same man with his face so serious and his hat gone. "Jonathan," he said solemnly, and when Jonathan met his eyes, stated, "We finish this."

Another scream of rage came from behind Jonathan, and he turned, backing towards Cecil, his Sig Sauer and knife ready. The tears had ceased; in their absence, all that remained was white-hot rage. "I'll kill you! I'll kill you! You're going to *die*," Jonathan screamed into the night.

There was a racket from the trees, and the wendigo leapt into the clearing, neatly covering the twenty feet to Jonathan and Cecil.

However, as it landed, they didn't give it any chance to move. Jonathan fired as fast as he could, but he couldn't match Cecil's speed. It was a quick *bam-bam,* pause, *bam-bam.*

The wendigo took a few steps back and screeched. Jonathan answered with a roar and put his last bullet into the wendigo's head, which snapped back. Then, without thinking about it, Jonathan tensed his muscles and with a flick of his wrist threw his knife.

Jonathan watched it turn end over end in the air three times before the knife sank to the hilt in the murderous creature's chest. The wendigo fell back with a gurgle and a spray of blood from its hated mouth.

Jonathan and Cecil ran forward, both reloading as fast as they could. But before Jonathan had even gotten his clip out, Cecil snapped both guns up with a jerk and began to fire into the downed wendigo again and again. Jonathan stepped up next to Cecil and began to empty his own clip into the enemy, but one of its huge feet kicked out and knocked Jonathan and Cecil back.

Wheezing and clawing at the ground, the wendigo tried to rise, but his head snapped to one side, and then part of his skull was just gone.

A half second later, the report of a rifle came to them.

"The gas," yelled Cecil, putting two more rounds into the gaunt chest of the creature that had fallen back to the ground. Its horrible hands covering its hideous, bleeding face.

Suddenly, Cory and Trevor ran up behind Jonathan and poured two large buckets of fuel onto the monster. Cecil spat on the wendigo. Putting away his right gun, he drew out a gold lighter.

"Burn in hell!" yelled Jonathan. The lighter flicked once, and Cecil tossed it down onto the scrabbling form at their feet.

Then, Jonathan shot the screaming creature twice as it literally lit up like a bonfire. The thing that once was the wendigo screamed and thrashed about. Jonathan wanted to kick and pummel it until it was dust. However, as Jonathan stepped forward to kick it, Cecil grabbed him and held him back. Jonathan struggled to get loose, but Cecil's grip was firm. Even when Jonathan punched the older man once in the stomach, his grip did not loosen.

Jonathan cried and howled at the heavens. He would tear them down if he could only reach them. Then Cecil spoke, "It's all right, lad. It's all over now." He kept saying it over and over again, holding Jonathan as he cried his rage and sadness out.

Finally, Jonathan looked up at the sound of wood sizzling. Cory and Trevor were keeping the fire going to make sure nothing was left of the wendigo. As Jonathan went to get some wood, he also saw Cecil wrap his hands in a cloth and pull Jonathan's knife out of the fire. "I'll have to thank him later for remembering the knife," thought Jonathan out loud.

Walking back to the fire with a bunch of dead branches, Jonathan saw his mother approaching from the direction of the amphitheater. Suddenly, she broke into a run, actually dropping her gun in the dirt. Jonathan ran to her and completely broke down in her arms. She was crying, too. His mother already knew that the love of her life was gone.

Then Cory's high voice broke the night like a knife: "I need help over here—now!" His voice came from the woods, which he had disappeared into to gather more branches. Jonathan and his mother looked at each other and then sprinted in the direction his voice had come from, with Cecil following closely behind.

They found Cory astonishingly at Jonathan's father's side. Barbara pushed past and began checking her husband's pulse. "His pulse is weak but still there," she said, worry and hope making her voice quiver.

"It won't be for long if we can't stop the bleeding," berated Cecil. He was on his knees next to Jonathan's father, peeling off his own shirt to wrap it around Adam's leg, trying to curb the bleeding. But the leg had been badly mangled, and bone poked through the skin. Blood continuously poured from the large wound, as big as one of Jonathan's hands, despite Cecil's efforts.

"I think it got the femoral artery. Barbara, apply pressure while I tie a tourniquet." Jonathan watched in horror as the two worked over his father, desperately trying to slow the bleeding.

"Somone call nine-one-one!" Cecil yelled out. "Tell them we have a severely injured man and a few dead."

Cory shook himself and pulled out his phone and made the call. Jonathan couldn't do anything; he felt helpless again. He would only get in the way if he tried to help. Then, his mother snapped at him, "Jonathan, keep his leg elevated."

Jonathan leapt forward to help. His father groaned in pain as Jonathan lifted the wounded leg as gently as he could. At the same time, Cecil finished the tourniquet and pulled it tight. Suddenly, Jonathan heard a strange whirring sound. Without pause, Cecil pulled out one of his guns, pointed in the air, and fired. The gun roared, and they all looked up to see something small and smoking plummet from the dark sky.

"Take care of him, Barbara. I have to make sure the drone is destroyed. She nodded, her eyes full of tears. With that, Cecil hurried off at a run. As he went, Jonathan took stock of Cecil's obviously strong back, but what grabbed his attention was the multitude of scars that covered it. The scars were varied in size and shape, consisting of everything from thin and thick lines to white scars the size of quarters. Then, the darkness and the foliage swallowed him.

Trevor came over to help Barbara apply pressure to Adam's leg. "We did it, at least," he said. Jonathan nodded, thinking that if his father died because he had left him behind to run, then the killing of the wendigo was not worth it. He would have to bring back the wendigo a hundred or a thousand times to kill it again, and it still would not be worth his father's life.

The minutes blurred together until finally, they heard the ambulance in the distance. Still, Barbara never relaxed her grip on her husband's leg, even when the paramedics got to them and started working. She didn't release her grip until they lifted her husband onto a brace, his face so white he already appeared to be a ghost. With Cory and Trevor bringing up the rear, Jonathan and his mother ran after the paramedics as they rushed to the ambulance.

Jonathan turned as the ambulance drove away, his mother riding with them. Jonathan knew she would stay by his father's side until he was awake again. There were six police cars now in the parking lot. The officers stood talking to the beer-bellied chief with Cecil shirtless at his side. Jonathan couldn't hear what they were saying. In fact, all sounds were coming to him as though he were underwater. His head felt like it was swaying on the deck of a ship. Then, as suddenly as lightning, the ground rushed up to meet him, and the world went black.

CHAPTER 21

Jonathan awoke to the soft beating of a cardiac monitor. He forced his eyes open and sat up, but even as he did so, his head swam, and he fell back onto his pillow. A voice spoke next to him, "Easy, lad, you're in the hospital. We had a bit of a wild night, didn't we?"

Looking around, the boy found Cecil sitting next to him, bathed in the morning sunlight. Jonathan slowly remembered. "Where's my dad?" he said in a rush.

"Still in surgery, but he's going to make it. Your mother is waiting for him."

Jonathan lay back and asked as calmly as he could, "What happened?"

"You fainted. Not surprising at your age and having gone through everything you did. Your friends, much to their displeasure, were picked up and taken home thirty minutes ago. I've already spoken to them. All that is left is for me and you to talk and finish things."

"But my—" Jonathan started, but Cecil rushed on.

"Your father fractured his femur along with his pelvis." Cecil looked tired and actually sat slumped in a hospital chair. He had taken the time to procure a mint-green dress shirt and a hunter-green waistcoat. His fedora sat forlornly on a rack by the door. "Overall, those injuries are bad, not to mention the beast cut him open, but also his femur punctured his femoral artery. He will be lucky if he can walk again at all," he finished sadly.

Jonathan sat there in shock. He did not know how to process what he'd just heard. So, for a few minutes, he sat in silence. He looked out the window, and the morning sun stung his eyes. He hurriedly wiped them to find them wet with tears. Then, a cardinal flew into view. It was so vibrant and alive. For a moment, he just watched it.

Finally, the bird flew away, and he asked, "What is it you need from me?"

"I need you to come with me. If I'm right about my hypothesis, then you will need to see what I suspect."

"What is it you suspect?"

"I won't say here. Let's just get out of here and finish this together."

At the last word, Jonathan looked at Cecil, who had a hand outstretched for Jonathan to take. Jonathan did, and then he pressed a button to call a nurse so they could get out of there.

It took them the majority of an hour before they received Jonathan's discharge papers. Before they left, though, Jonathan wanted to check on his mother and father.

Walking into the waiting room, Jonathan saw his mother pacing. When she caught sight of him, she hurried over and pulled him into a rib-cracking hug. "Hun, you're out of bed. How are you feeling?" she asked, looking deep into his eyes.

"I'm fine now. How's Dad?"

She looked back at the doors through which Jonathan knew his father was still in surgery. Her eyes were tired, with big bags under them. "The doctors think they can save his leg. However, there may be some nerve damage," she said, sounding completely worn out.

Jonathan took a breath. "At least he will be okay. Will you let me know when he wakes up?"

"You're not staying?" Her voice was full of concern.

Jonathan looked away, not wanting to meet her eyes. "I've got to finish this," he said simply.

"Cecil," she started darkly, a tick starting at her eyebrow, which was always a bad sign. Then she surprised them both; she blew out a breath and said to her son, "Just be careful, and keep the presents we gave you close."

"Thanks, Mom," he said. He hugged her and, before he started crying like a little kid, turned away to meet up with Cecil.

Jonathan was surprised when Cecil picked him up in the family van. "Figured Adam wouldn't mind if I borrowed this. Especially considering what we need it for."

Jonathan got in and fastened his seat belt. "What are we doing? Isn't it about time you at least told me?"

Cecil smiled and answered, "No."

"Why not?"

"I want you to come to the same conclusion as I did with an unbiased point of view."

That was all he would say. And Jonathan couldn't find it in him to fill the silence with pointless talking. He was still so tired; he closed his eyes.

Too soon, they were pulling back up at Sodalis Nature Preserve. The scene had been cleared of remnants of the night's events. Jonathan was surprised when he saw there were no police at the scene, keeping people out or investigating. He looked at Cecil, his eyebrows raised in question.

Cecil laughed, "If you come to work with us at GCAC, you will also have a few good benefits. It's not just monster hunting. There is more to it than that. We also have to manage the aberrant biological creatures. Some of that is keeping in contact with some of the more sentient of those."

"Biological aberrants? What are those?"

"Come work for us and find out, lad," Cecil said, winking.

Turning off the van, Cecil climbed out, followed by Jonathan. Jonathan didn't know where to start. Then, Cecil said, "Come on, lad. On the hop."

He led Jonathan over to the spot where they had burned the wendigo. "One thing you always do as a monster hunter is check to confirm the monster is really dead."

"This looks pretty dead," said Jonathan, gesturing at the small pile of ash. Cecil took no notice but started rustling through it.

"So . . . is he dead?" asked Jonathan with a bit of a smirk on his face.

Cecil frowned at him deeply for once. "Never jump to conclusions, especially with the abnormal. This case has been full of plenty of things that go the way they shouldn't. A wendigo that heals faster than a vampire is definitely not right. Then, you have its actions. I've been on more cases than anyone alive, most of them with Adam. This is the first time a monster has gotten the drop on him, not once, but twice!"

Jonathan took a step back, a little shocked.

"My apologies, Master Campbell. I'm afraid my emotions are out of sorts. It's not every day, even for me, that a warrior and hunter like your father goes down."

Jonathan looked away and simply nodded. Then, to break the heavy silence, he asked again, "Is it dead?"

"It appears so," Cecil answered, frowning. Then he turned away, his manner changing. "Time for you to do what your father could do so well. It's time to track down where the monster lived."

"How do I do that?"

"Well, we follow the blood trail and narrow down which mine entrance he used." Pulling out a map of the preserve, he pointed out the multitude of mine entrances. There were thirty-three in total.

"Do we have to check all of them?" asked Jonathan.

"No, we use our little gray cells, lad," Cecil said, pointing to his head. Then, he went on, "Which of these would not be accessible to the general public? You live here; you know these entrances, don't you?" Jonathan nodded, looking hard at the map.

The majority of the entrances could be accessed via the many trails that ran throughout the two-hundred-acre preserve. However, in the woods were a handful of smaller entrances that were not as grandiose as the primary ones. Jonathan pointed to their locations on the map and said, "These spots should be our best bet."

"Well then, let's get going," said Cecil, turning away. Jonathan walked after him into the woods.

Cecil used his cane often to move aside low-hanging limbs. They walked together in silence until Jonathan couldn't hold back questions any longer. "How long were my parents hunters? And how long have you been a hunter?"

Cecil grinned, and his blue eyes danced with merriment. "I have been a hunter for a long time. However, a gentleman like me likes to keep his age under wraps."

"What about my parents?" asked Jonathan, undeterred.

"Your parents helped me for around fifteen years . . . after your grandfather retired for a much-deserved rest."

Jonathan stopped in his tracks. "My grandfather helped you?" He had heard that his grandfather, who had died five years ago, had been a hunter, although he hadn't known at the time exactly what kind of hunter. "How long did you hunt with my grandfather?"

Cecil turned and grinned again at Jonathan. "A long time. You have quite the hunter's pedigree, Master Campbell."

Cecil turned on his heels, saying, "Come on, now. We must find this monster's lair."

Jonathan followed after Cecil, wondering just how old the mysterious man was. He appeared to be in the prime of his life. Was Cecil even a normal human? Doing some mental math, Jonathan found the numbers just did not add up for a man in his mid-thirties or early forties. Jonathan walked after Cecil, puzzled about what his story could be. But the thing that mattered was that both his parents and grandfather had trusted this man enough to work with him. Therefore, he would too.

They continued to make their way through the woods, and Jonathan explained about the caves he had pointed out. "The caves that aren't popular spots for sightseeing become good spots for teens to hang out in, or for people—like Trevor's friend Neal—who love bats to get an uninterrupted view of the bats coming out."

Cecil moved like a wildcat, making as little noise as Jonathan did; he was used to then moving through the woods quietly. "Okay, but what about the other spots that aren't local hangouts?"

Jonathan stopped for a moment, asking, "Can I see the map again?"

Without question, Cecil pulled it out and opened it once more. Jonathan pointed a finger at cave entrance number thirty-two. "I never even knew about this cave entrance."

Cecil nodded his understanding. "Therefore, this number thirty-two is a more hidden entrance. Maybe that was hidden for a reason." Jonathan nodded his agreement and continued trekking through the woods. Cecil was pushing past a bush when Jonathan grabbed his arm in shock. Cecil froze and looked back at Jonathan with concern. Jonathan simply pointed to the red-stained leaves to their left.

"Good eye, Master Campbell. We appear to be on the right track."

Jonathan tried to grin, but it was hard not to think of how much blood had been bled to stain those leaves red like that. It made Jonathan a little green just thinking about it. Walking on more slowly now, with their eyes sharp, they went about thirty feet further through the woods . . . and found a body.

Jonathan did his best not to look at the lifeless form to see who it had been. He did not want to look weak in front of Cecil.

"It appears to be a young adult. Many of the internal organs show evidence of having been eaten, of course."

Jonathan, though, was looking at some foliage that had been hacked down with a sharp blade. "Cecil, take a look at this."

Cecil hurried over, and Jonathan watched his face as he took in the mangled plants. He ran a practiced hand in a slow, slashing movement that a blade must have taken. "Good eye," Cecil complimented him again. "Must have been a heavy blade to break these branches. Probably done by a machete or something like it."

"What does that mean, though?" asked Jonathan.

"It means someone else was looking for our hidden cave entrance."

Jonathan glanced around hard and noticed several spots of cut brush. Cecil followed Jonathan's gaze and nodded, something apparently proven to him.

"What does this mean?" asked Jonathan again.

"It means a team of people moved through. And I think they had a purpose with our friend wendigo." Then Cecil began to follow the obvious path that the mangled brush gave them. After another five minutes, they came across a gun covered in blood. Jonathan didn't know what type of gun it was, but it looked military.

"It's a Myers bullpup, definitely not your ordinary bushman."

"What were these people doing here?" Jonathan wondered aloud.

"Hold your questions, lad; answers are up ahead," said Cecil, gesturing to the open cave entrance. They both approached at a trot. The bars that had gone horizontally had clearly been cut. Unlike most of the entrances, which were large, gaping ones, this entrance was barely five feet tall. The edges of the remaining bars were clean cut. However, they were caked in old blood, so they appeared rusted.

"Whoever they were," Jonathan commented, "I don't think many of them got away clean."

"I agree. The available evidence would suggest that we are going into a bit of a bloodfest."

They met eyes, and Cecil took the lead, pulling out one of his guns and a small, thin flashlight. Jonathan pulled out his own gun and followed him inside. As in most caves, their footsteps echoed around, sounding like multitudes of people walking. However, unlike most caves, which could be damp, the Sodalis caves were quite dry. Though the entrance had been small, Jonathan was at least able to walk unhunched.

Cecil kept his light low, careful not to disturb any of the cave's inhabitants.

"How often does the GCAC have to step in to resolve issues with, as you call them, aberrant species?"

"All the time," said Cecil with a sigh. "However, you get to go places all over the world and see things nobody else gets to."

"Like what?" asked Jonathan, trying yet failing to hide his excitement.

"Well, for instance, controlling the news of thunderbirds."

"There actually are thunderbirds?" Jonathan half shouted, his voice magnified in the cave.

Chiding himself and trying to ignore Cecil's grin, he asked more softly, "There really are thunderbirds?"

"Of course. For the most part, they live far from people, deep in the wilderness. So it's really just meeting with people who do happen to see them and politely asking them not to blab about the creatures."

They paused as they rounded a corner to find a bloody mess. At first, it was hard to say if this had once been human or not. Then, Jonathan saw a head. His stomach lurched, and he barely held back his vomit.

"Are you going to be okay to continue?" Cecil asked. "It will only get worse from here."

Jonathan only nodded, and Cecil gave him a pat on the shoulder before leading them around the sickening remnants of violence.

As they rounded another corner, the cave path opened up into a vast cavern of a room. Jonathan did throw up this time as bodies were everywhere—how many, he didn't want to know. Cecil began closely inspecting each of the corpses.

Jonathan closed his eyes, took a deep breath, and reopened them to see Cecil holding another blood-covered Myers bullpup. He checked for rounds and stated, "Empty. Whoever they were, they went down fighting."

Jonathan looked about the room, trying not to focus on anything until his eyes caught the glint of tarnished metal.

"Over there," he pointed, and they both hurried in that direction. On the far wall, bolted to the rock, were four sizeable old chains. Jonathan picked one up and looked at its broken end. "These were sawed through, just like the bars at the entrance. But why would people do something like this?"

"Because of these."

Jonathan turned to look at Cecil. He held a half dozen large needles.

"What the hell?" shouted Jonathan.

"Yes, this is what I feared. Someone deliberately set the wendigo free to run an experiment.

Thirty minutes later, they were back in the van. Jonathan had ranted, unloading his anger and disgust on Cecil, who had calmly taken it all until Jonathan's temper was finally spent. Now he asked, "Master Campbell, will you join the GCAC? If you do, you can help us stop people like this."

All Jonathan said was, "Drive me home, please. I need to pick up a book."

Cecil drove over the roads in record time. At one point, Jonathan checked the speedometer to see they were nearly going fifty on the park's rough roads. However, they did not see any police. In fact, they did not see much of anyone. Jonathan wondered if the gun shots and events of last night had frightened everyone into staying indoors.

"Where do you—"

"Think everyone is?" finished Cecil. Jonathan nodded. Cecil grinned at him from under his fedora. "For one thing, it's a Saturday. It is my understanding that most people rise late on Saturdays. For another thing, the police, at my suggestion, made an announcement that a rabid bear was caught and humanely euthanized."

"So that's it, a bear with rabies? And people buy that type of lie?"

"Of course. Most people want to know that they are safe. Do the details really matter? No. As long as the thing that was attacking people is dead is all that matters to most people."

Jonathan said, "If it were up to me, I would always prefer the truth."

"But that's where people like you and me are different. We want to know everything that lurks in the darkness."

A minute or so later, they pulled up outside of the Campbells' empty house. Jonathan wondered how his dad was doing and if he was out of surgery yet. He would have to go there after he collected the book. Pushing open the front door, he led Cecil through to the kitchen and down into the basement. He did his best to ignore Cecil's curious glances around the interior. It was as though a home like this was unfamiliar to him. Finally, Jonathan asked, "Don't you have a house of your own?"

"Of course I do. I have several houses. However, I don't have anywhere that I would truly call home. Not since the war."

"The war? Which war?"

"It doesn't matter; it is a story for another time. Now, let's get that book," said Cecil, gesturing to the room.

Getting on his hands and knees, Jonathan crawled under the pool table and to the far leg. The hollow was right where his father had said it would be. From inside, he pulled out a large, beat-up notebook wrapped in old leather, maybe deer hide.

Rolling out from under the table, he swiftly stood up and set the book down on it.

"Ah, that book. I understand now," Cecil commented with a slow nod.

"You know about my father's book?" asked Jonathan.

"Of course. He often brought it with him on hunts."

Taking a deep breath, Jonathan opened the book to find his father's handwriting along with another person's. It said, *Inside this book is the legacy of hunters. This is the work of the Campbell family.* At the bottom were his father's and his grandfather's signatures.

Jonathan closed the book and gripped his eyes tightly shut. This was his book now, and he would use it to hunt the creatures of the world that needed hunting. He would protect those people who needed protection. And he would find the people who had used his town and its people as some lame experiment. Looking up at Cecil, he matter-of-factly said, "I'm in."

ABOUT THE AUTHOR

Growing up in the heartland of Missouri, author Benjamin Coward first discovered the thrill of world-building through role-playing games like Dungeons and Dragons and books in The Inheritance Cycle series by Christopher Paolini. In his YA fantasy novels, Benjamin masterfully creates realms where relatable characters fight evil opponents and overcome struggles through teamwork and self-trust. With a bachelor's degree in environmental science and now living and working in north central Florida, Benjamin's love of nature and history often seep into his storytelling, enriching the fantastical yet believable worlds he creates.